THE LION'S SHARE

ROBERT CAMPBELL

THE MYSTERIOUS PRESS

Published by Warner Books

A Time Warner Company

MYSTERIOUS PRESS EDITION

Copyright © 1996 by Robert Campbell
All rights reserved.

Cover design by Jackie Merri Meyer
Cove illustration by Nicolas Gaetano

The Mysterious Press name and logo are registered trademarks of Warner Books, Inc.

 Mysterious Press Books are published by
Warner Books, Inc.
1271 Avenue of the Americas
New York, NY 10020

Visit our Web site at
http://pathfinder.com/twep

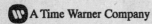 A Time Warner Company

Printed in the United States of America

Originally published in hardcover by The Mysterious Press.
First Printed in Paperback: June, 1997
10 9 8 7 6 5 4 3 2 1

Novels by Robert Campbell

<u>THE JIMMY FLANNERY SERIES</u>
The Junkyard Dog • *The 600 Pound Gorilla* • *Hip-Deep in Alligators* • *The Cat's Meow* • *Thinning the Turkey Herd* • *Nibbled to Death by Ducks* • *The Gift Horse's Mouth* • *In a Pig's Eye* • *Sauce for the Goose* • *The Lion's Share*

<u>THE WHISTLER SERIES</u>
In La-La Land We Trust • *Alice in La-La Land* • *Sweet La-La Land* • *The Wizard of La-La Land*

<u>THE JAKE HATCH SERIES</u>
Plugged Nickel • *Red Cent*

<u>OTHER CRIME NOVELS</u>
Honor • *Juice* • *Boneyards*

<u>WRITING AS R. WRIGHT CAMPBELL</u>
The Spy Who Sat and Waited • *Circus Couronne* • *Where Pigeons Go to Die* • *Killer of Kings* • *Malloy's Subway* • *Fat Tuesday*

<u>WRITING AS F.G. CLINTON</u>
The Tin Cop

Dedicated to the staff of the Harrison Memorial Library,
the best little book-house in California

THE LION'S
SHARE

1

My name's Jimmy Flannery. I'm so used to saying that up front, the occupation that I'm in, that sometimes I forget and stick out my hand and say, "Hi, I'm Jimmy Flannery," to people I've known for twenty years.

My old man, Mike, who's crowding seventy, laughs when he catches me doing that and lets everybody know that he's getting worried about a son that's so forgetful.

"With some people it's the memory that goes first, not the legs," he says.

He could be right, though I got an idea my generation don't exercise our memories the way his generation exercised theirs, what with all the databases and speed dials and watches that buzz you when it's time to call your wife.

I hate to think what the next generation's going to do if they find themselves stranded somewheres without their cellular phones or notebook computers; they'll probably just stand there going through the alphabet, the way Mrs. Brody in the fifth grade taught us to do to try and jog our memories, in hopes that a letter will remind them of their own name.

Also it has to do with how many people you meet from day to day and under what circumstances. I mean a lot of people don't meet more than one person they got to remember for the future in a week.

They could meet hundreds every day . . . nodding and smiling and saying how are you? . . . like the checker at the supermarket, which is outside my neighborhood, where I buy my staples. I'll bet we've said hello a thousand times but never even passed the time of day. She's busy and the boss is pushing her and she just wants you to keep moving along so she can do her seven and a half and go on home to rest her feet. Also she's not required to recognize you on the street, so she probably won't.

Not like Joe and Pearl what own the grocery store downstairs in the five-family and a shop building where me and my wife, Mary, and our little girl, Kathleen, live. Sometimes when I go in there for a quart of milk or a loaf of bread, it's an hour before I can get away, because we talk, me and Joe and Pearl and the customers.

They tell me their troubles, first because I try to listen, and second because I been a worker in the precincts since 1978, a precinct captain in the Twenty-seventh for fourteen years and the committeeman, which is like the ward leader for the Democratic Party, for five. Eighteen years in Chicago politics, which I love altogether.

Being a party worker ain't my paid job. For wages I put in forty hours a week as a sewer inspector in the Sewer Department under Streets and Sanitation. Before I became an inspector I walked the tunnels for ten years and that was no fun.

I owe both of these careers to Chips Delvin, who's been my Chinaman since he got me my first job in the sewers and my first assignment knocking on doors for the party at election time. For which I'm very grateful. Though I don't thank him very often for putting me down in the sewers the way he done.

But I got a feeling that what you end up doing chooses
you as much as you choose it.

Anyway, after he kind of anointed me his heir in a
half-assed sort of way, I'm halfway to becoming him, because although I ain't head of the Sewer Department like
he was for almost forty years, I am the committeeman for
the ward in which I live. I probably never will be the superintendent of sewers what with these talent searches
they have for department heads where they interview kids
with degrees just fresh out of college.

I'm doing what I can to improve myself, taking classes
in adult education, working toward a degree in the great
by-and-by, but it's a slow way of doing it. One of these
days I'll just have to bite the bullet and carry a full
course load of credits in some community college I could
afford.

I was thinking maybe city management, or political
science, or that good old standby for everybody looking
to climb the political ladder . . . the law.

When Delvin and Dunleavy, who could be even a couple of years older than Delvin and runs Streets and Sanitation for even longer than Delvin runs the sewers, was
starting out, it was more favor for favor than it is today,
especially after the Shankman court decree which out-
lawed political hiring and firing, taking most city jobs out
from under political influence. Though it ain't possible to
rule out that way of doing business altogether and still
say this is the city that works. There's always somebody
ready to cut the corner, bend the angle and wink the eye
and I ain't sure that's always and altogether a bad thing.

I'm sitting by the open window in the kitchen on a summer morning on my day off, making like a horsey with
my daughter on my knee, the *Tribune* in one hand and
eating cereal with two percent milk with the other, when
Mary asks me what I'm thinking about.

Whenever one of us asks the other one what's on our

mind we don't duck the question, we try to answer it. When it's something off the wall, we even try to trace the thought back to see what could have triggered it.

So I tell her I was thinking of these old-timers and what it was like when they was young, me thinking of them as being young, though I'm about the same age they was then but feeling kind of middle-aged right that minute.

"You're not that old," Mary says.

"I didn't say old, I said middle-aged."

It's funny the way we talk about different ages and getting older. I mean the way it is nowadays you're just starting into middle age when you reach seventy. So when you maybe kick off a couple of years later everybody says, my God, such a young person.

Mary takes Kathleen from me and puts her in the high chair because Kathleen has a tendency to get overexcited playing horsey.

"How would you measure middle age, Jimmy?" she asks.

"All right, let's say it's like in the Bible, human beings live roughly three score and then. Seventy years, give or take. So half of seventy is thirty-five, right in the middle. From when you're born to the age of ten, you could call that childhood. I won't count that because you're learning what you need to know to start operating even a little bit. So, okay, we'll move the middle to forty."

"That's all right with me," Mary says.

"From ten to twenty, we're in our youth. Twenty to thirty, young adulthood. Thirty to fifty, middle age."

"You doubled up there, Jimmy," she says.

"Well, if forty's the middle, I'm taking ten years on either side."

"So fifty to sixty, you're in your maturity," I says.

"Most people would call fifty to sixty pretty young, but I wouldn't mind it said of me that I was in my maturity when I turn fifty," she says.

"Well, that's a whole new factor we got there. They say a man peaks sexually when he's eighteen or twenty. A woman's in her prime when she reaches thirty-five or forty. So the way you could look at it is—"

"You'll be all used up just when I'm about to work up an appetite."

"Maybe we shouldn't be talking like this in front of Kathleen," I says.

"Oh, yes, I'm sure she's taking notes. So, all right, if you're happier analyzing chronological age instead of sexual ability, go ahead."

"Sixty to seventy you're in your old age, although you might not be anywhere near gaga," I says.

"Not everybody goes gaga," she says, sticking her oar in there.

"By the time you're seventy you're in old age and at eighty you're ancient," I goes on. "At ninety I can't imagine."

"There's some talk about moving the traditional year of retirement up to seventy-five," she says. "People living so much longer is one of the reasons why Medicare is going broke and Social Security apt to do so down the line."

"Well, I got nothing against that. At least I don't think I do," I says.

"What got you thinking about all this?" she asks.

"Well, like I said, I was thinking about Delvin and Dunleavy."

"But what got you thinking about them?"

"I was thinking I might go over to see my old China-man this morning and maybe even go over to Streets and Sanitation to see Dunleavy this afternoon, even though I ain't got a favor to ask from him. On the other hand, it might give him a shock, me visiting without a favor to ask, so maybe I better not."

The phone rings and I go answer it.

It's Mrs. Thimble, Delvin's housekeeper.

"Can you come over right away, Mr. Flannery?" she says. "Mr. Delvin passed away in his sleep during the night. I found him ten minutes ago when I went in to bring him his tea."

"Oh, dear," I says, mostly to myself, "I hope this ain't the short beginning to a long ending."

I don't know what makes me say that, except that Delvin's done a lot of borderline things in his long career and I'm hoping, now that he's gone, a whole bunch of skeletons don't come dancing out of his closet.

2

It's beautiful summer weather outside when I go over to Delvin's old house on Aberdeen in Bridgeport, which along with Canaryville is in the Eleventh Ward. It was the old Mayor's neighborhood all his life and Delvin's neighborhood, too.

It's a holdout ward and a holdout neighborhood. By which I mean going into Bridgeport is like going into one end of a time machine and out the other. It's a neighborhood what's got a history what's intact. It's everywhere you look, in the frame houses and brick bungalows, the solid old Catholic churches anchoring the faith, and the taverns like Schaller's Pump at Thirty-seventh and Halsted right across the street from ward Democratic Headquarters.

There's white-haired men inside who'll tell you tales their fathers told them about how the Irish, unable to vote back home under English rule, took to politics like ducks to water and elected first John Hopkins in the 1880s and then Edward Dunne, who took the mayor's seat in 1905 and warmed it for two years.

How settlers built houses along the south branch of the

river, which was later, after the stockyards went in, called Bubbly Creek because of the gas produced by rotting carcasses, and in a place called Hardscrabble or the Cabbage Patch because everybody grew cabbages for the pot.

It got to be called Bridgeport because there was this low bridge crossing the river at Ashland the barges couldn't pass underneath, so the barges had to unload one side and reload onto new barges the other.

Sometimes I wonder who the wise guy was what built that low bridge and how he probably lined his pockets by doing it.

And they'll tell you stories they was eyewitness to, or actually involved in, about Ed Kelly, who took office in 1933, after Anton Cermak was assassinated in the attempt on Franklin Delano Roosevelt, some saying Cermak was the target all along, and sat there on top of a pile of favors and deals until they kicked him out in '47 because he went too far.

But the hero of most of the tales is the late Richard J. Daley, the Democratic Party's and the Irishmen's finest flower.

Daley "maintained the mood" of Bridgeport, they say, by excluding blacks, even building the Dan Ryan Expressway, they say, keeping Bridgeport and Canaryville separate from the black wards. It remains so still.

I ain't going to make an argument for or against segregation of wards or neighborhoods, schools or churches, or any other public institution or facility for that matter. I don't live that way, but I ain't going to say something which always upsets me whenever I hear it said. I ain't going to say some of my best friends is African Americans because that's more like saying you harbor some feelings of prejudice and feel you got to deny it by saying such a thing. Showing what a nice liberal person you are.

I've been in the homes of people with every color and shade of skin you can name, and sat down to a meal with them, and cried with them when they was hurting, and sat up with their dead, but now I got to say something else which is also true. I get a sweet, funny feeling when I go into Bridgeport. Not that I believe that business about the past being basically gentler or more innocent. But I want to believe it and I get this good feeling when I go over to Delvin's even on such a sorrowful occasion.

I'm already thinking about what funeral arrangements I'm going to have to make because I don't know who else is going to do it.

Mrs. Thimble meets me at the door. She's so upset, though she's trying not to show it, that she don't even scold me for not wiping my feet or anything like that.

The hallway don't smell as dusty and musty as it usually smells. It smells of candle wax and sage so I know she's lit some candles to put at the head and foot of his bed, and burned some spices in a dish to mask the odor of death which some people claim they can smell a mile away.

"You call the doctor?" I asks.

"No, I called you," she says.

"You happen to know his doctor's number offhand?" I asks.

She rattles it off to me and adds, "He lives just down the block."

I dial the number on the old rotary phone and Dr. Squertsky himself picks up.

"This is Jimmy Flannery," I says.

"Delvin's friend?" he says.

"That's right. Mr. Delvin passed away during the night."

"I'm not surprised. It could have happened any minute."

"I'm about to call the undertaker and I'll need a death certificate."

"Give me ten minutes and I'll be right over."

I hang up and start on what comes next.

"You happen to know what undertaker Mr. Delvin wanted to lay him out?"

"When he mentioned it at all, he said we should tear up

the floor in the corner of Schallert's Pump and bury him under it in a beer barrel. It was a joke. He didn't mean it."

"I think you're right. So he never said who he'd like to do the honors?"

"Well, there was one time when he joked about how Lou Cleary—"

"The cop," I says, not wanting to interrupt, but merely indicating I know the gentleman in question.

"—was retiring from the force and how he was going to go into his son-in-law's—"

"Jackie Diversey," I says, by way of naming the connection.

"—undertaking business," she goes right on, taking no offense at me commenting while she's talking. "He thought it might be nice to throw a little business Cleary's way, he said."

"I wonder did he think there was a way to get back a favor for the favor?" I says, half to myself, remembering that O'Shea, this homicide cop what don't like me very much or at least does a very good job of pretending he don't, is married to Jackie Diversey's sister. So what you got is you got an awful lot of cops what got connections with this funeral parlor to which a lot of business finds its way.

Cleary had been in Homicide when he retired, though I don't think he was ever teamed with O'Shea, but before that the older cop had been Vice.

Rumor had it that in those days he'd often shield selected ladies from the consequences of arrest, taking their markers to be called in at his convenience later on, working police smokers and bachelors parties on the cheap. It was also rumored that he not only kept contact with these professional ladies but that, after retirement, he more or less formalized an arrangement with them whereby he continued to get them dates and social engagements, taking a percentage of their compensation to supplement his pension.

This on top of helping out his son-in-law in the undertaking business, Cleary being one of them people who always likes to have several sources of income.

It wasn't outside the realm of possibility that Delvin, once upon a time, had desired the tender mercies of some lady on occasion and had cut a deal with Cleary, trading favor for favor.

I don't mention any of this to Mrs. Thimble, who was once the housekeeper for a priest and shouldn't know about such things, though she probably knows more about such things than me, being the housekeeper of a priest and then a politician of some fame.

"Well," I says, "If he didn't say so in writing or give definite instructions to somebody he trusted, like yourself," I says, "I suppose Diversey's it'll be."

She holds a finger in the air, marking something she's just remembered.

"Mr. Delvin used to remind me practically once a day that if anything was to happen to him, I was to bring you the mahogany document box he kept in the chiffonier."

"Let's see what we can see," I says, and follow her down the dark hallway to Delvin's bedroom, where, just as I expected, candles are burning at the head and foot of the bed in which he's laying with his hands neatly folded on his chest on top of a pile of blankets, like he'd been cold in the night like old people get no matter how warm it is.

His eyes is closed, with two shinny copper pennies on them, which is an old custom. I swear to God it gives me the funniest feeling because one of the pennies ain't quite in line with the others and it looks like he's winking at me.

The smell of burnt sage is heavier in this room and I'm afraid it's going to make me sneeze.

I open the door to the chiffonier and nearly fall over backwards because I forget these old-fashioned pieces of furniture usually has a full-length mirror in the door, just like this one has, which gives me back the reflections of a solemn, tight-lipped old woman, a white-faced, redheaded man and a winking corpse propped up on pillows.

I pick up the box on the floor of the bureau and says, "Let's take this into the parlor, where we won't be disturbed."

Mrs. Thimble gives me a funny look like she's afraid I'm one of them what believes in ghosts. Or maybe she believes in ghosts, which is not unlikely, and thinks she's found somebody to talk about ghosts with.

We got into the parlor, where the green shades are pulled down to the sills from the night before and let them up so we can have a little natural light in the room, pushing aside the lace curtains that smell of age and dust. Then I sit in the chair opposite the one in which Delvin always sat, the afghan for his knees still folded over the back, pull up an end table, make room for the box, set it down and open it.

The smell of old paper money and tobacco hits me in the nose and I finally do sneeze.

"God bless you," Mrs. Thimble says, and raises her eyes to the ceiling as though expecting God to answer back.

Delvin turns out to be a very neat and orderly person. Everything anybody would need to attend to his affairs is there, filed in separate envelopes and pressed-cardboard report covers.

Every envelope is labeled with a title, which I can tell was typed out on the old Corona he kept in his office. I can't tell you how many times I see him pecking away on it with two fingers, his nose almost on the keys.

There's a fat envelope labeled "house inventory," another labeled "personal possessions," another that says "safe," and another that says "vehicles."

There's one addressed to Mrs. Thimble. One for Father Dietrich. One for somebody named Jane Paboojian.

I'm looking for a packet addressed to an attorney or a bank trustee but there ain't any.

However there's two for me. One says "Jimmy Flannery" and the other says "James Flannery, Trustee."

I don't know which one to open first. Then I figure the

one to Jimmy is probably going to be a personal letter and the other all business, so I figure I got to take care of first things first.

It gives me a funny feeling taking the pages out, like I expect to hear his voice scolding me for nosing into his private business before being invited.

What the top page of a seven-page document says is that one Francis Brendan Delvin, being of sound mind, does name one James Barnabas Flannery his trustee and executor, such costs and fees for service to be calculated at ten percent of the appraised value of house and contents, stocks, bonds and other financial instruments, surrender value of insurance policies, cash in checking and savings accounts, plus cash in hand before taxes, but not including personal possessions, jewelry or paintings.

A spillover will moves cash in hand and monies in a checking account into a living trust which had been drawn up by Tom Hawley, Attorney. It's pretty obvious that was housekeeping money and Mrs. Thimble's wages for maybe three or four months.

A note paper-clipped to the page advises me that Hawley has already been paid his fee for services rendered and is standing by to give me any "ordinary advice," which warns me that I better watch what I ask him to do or the estate'll get hit with a bill.

There are a page of bequests, at the top of which was the transfer of the deed to the very house in which I'm standing. The house, furnishings and enough cash to cover transfer expenses goes to me, but only if me and my family actually occupy it for at least five years.

I suppose Delvin remembers how his last housekeeper, Mrs. Banjo, left me a vacant lot when she died and how me and Mary decided to sell instead of building on it so we could go into a partnership with the people in our building what wanted to buy it so we could keep on being neighbors.

Back then, there was the Recores, Mr. and Mrs. and

seven kids, five daughters—Maureen, the oldest, a roller skater—and two sons—the youngest, Stanley, a special friend of mine—what lived across the hall.

Just underneath my flat was Mrs. Warnowski, Mooshie Warnowski's widow, and next to her Myron and Shirley Shapiro, schoolteachers, and their little girl.

On the ground floor was Miss King and her companion Mrs. Foran.

The corner flat had been converted into a grocery store years ago and was owned by Pearl and Joe Pakula, who took care of their mother.

But that was seven years ago and plenty has changed since then, not only the building but the neighborhood.

The Recores still live there, the father retired and the mother marking time until she can talk him into moving out to California where three of her kids, two daughters and a son, are living. One of them, the oldest girl, the skater, was killed coming home from the skating rink. Shot in the head for the contents of her purse. They asked me to help find out who done it but neither me or the police ever could. Another daughter died of meningitis.

Stanley still lives at home. He's eighteen years old now. The speech impediment which made him so funny and endearing went away and he don't talk much at all any more, being mostly sullen and out of work. His brother's in prison in Texas, busted for dealing drugs, and the mother and father are afraid Stanley might follow in his footsteps.

They've had their share of troubles and sorrows, the Recores.

Mrs. Warnowski left to live with her sister out in Cicero shortly after Mooshie was made Fireman of the Year in a grand ceremony on the steps of the City Hall.

Mr. and Mrs. Bilina moved in right after and then Mr. Bilina died.

There was some fuss about getting him buried, him falling out of the coffin and all, being worshipped as a saint who had been seen to elevate right out of the grave, waving to the crowd on his way to heaven, and she still lives on the second floor across from the Shapiros.

Mrs. Bilina put up some of the life insurance money for her share of the building when we bought it back in '89 to keep it from getting flattened for new development, but now she's talking about moving out before the neighborhood gets any worse than it is, the new development never getting off the ground anyway.

The Shapiros also want a better place to raise their little girl. They've been looking for a buyer for their flat without any luck at all. The other day Myron told me he was ready to bail out even if all he could get was fifty cents on the dollar.

Which is how depressed neighborhoods get trashed out in the first place. But they figure they fought the good fight to save the neighborhood and now it's time to face the facts.

Both Miss King and Mrs. Forán is gone, passed away within two weeks of one another. Their ground-floor flat is rented by a black family, the Hensons. He's a police officer and she works down at the welfare office.

Joe and Pearl Pakula's mother died last year but the brother and sister are still running the grocery store. I used to wash my car from a hose hooked up to their outside tap every Saturday afternoon. People would stop by and talk to me about their needs and troubles. It was like my office.

But now that I'm the ward leader I used Alderman . . . woman . . . Janet Canarias's storefront once a week to meet with my constituents and listen to their complaints.

I ain't got time to wash my car at the tap outside Pakula's grocery store. When the car really needs it, I take it over to a car wash and pay my five bucks for a plain wash, no vacuum or wax.

Mary's forever saying things happen when they're meant to happen, which I don't believe but which I don't argue about. I believe stuff happens period, end of sentence, end of theory. Which is also not to say that I ain't also been thinking it's time to change our address. So, in that regard, this opportunity to move into a big house in Bridgeport is not altogether unwelcome, though I wished it didn't take the death of an old friend to get it done.

One other thing in the letter from Delvin. If I accept the house and furniture, I got to waive the executor's fee, which will then be pooled with the other resources and distributed according to the remainder of the bequest list. Which is only fair.

There's a knock at the front door. Mrs. Thimble don't seem to notice.

"There's somebody at the door," I says. "You want me to get it?"

"Oh, no," she says.

She gets up and leaves the room.

I put in a call to the Diversey Funeral Home.

The young woman who answers the phone cuts the difference between being mournful and cheerful better than anybody I ever heard.

When I tell her the name of the deceased, I can practically see her straighten up in her chair and I wonder if Cleary and Diversey have given her a list of names of people who may be calling on them for service any day.

"Let me see if Mr. Diversey himself is available," she says.

Dr. Squertsky comes in. He lives and has his office in his house just down the street, and he don't make house calls much any more, so he's wearing his bedroom slippers and a cardigan sweater with a stethoscope poking out of the pocket.

He gives me a nod and what passes for a hello. I give him the same, standing there with the phone to my ear.

Squertsky goes back into the downstairs bedroom to give Delvin a quick once-over.

Diversey, Cleary's son-in-law, who I've met more than once or twice, here and there, social functions such as fu-

nerals being right up there with weddings and christenings
as social events where practically everyone gathers, gets on
the line. He's got the voice of a professional mourner.

"Mr. Flannery," he says. "Jimmy. Did my daughter get it
right? Is it Chips Delvin who's gone to his reward?"

"It is," I says.

"I'm devastated by your loss. Thank you for calling me.
Let me tell you that I . . . we . . . all of us . . . will do our
very, very best for that dear old man."

You could call Delvin a lot of things but dear old man
ain't among them. He'd have wrestled Diversey to the floor
if he ever heard hisself spoken about like that.

"Are you calling from the hospital or is it from the house
of bereavement?" Diversey goes on.

"Delvin died at home in his bed during the night."

"Shall we come get him, then?"

"If you would."

"As soon as I can find my father-in-law. Lou's somewhere about. You know Lou Cleary?"

"Indeed I do."

"They were the best of friends, old Mr. Delvin and my
father-in-law. You also know my brother-in-law, Francis
O'Shea?"

"I do."

"It's like we're all family," Diversey says, and I'm half
tempted to ask him will the relationship be reflected on the
bill.

"We'll be waiting for you," I says.

"Ahhh," Diversey sighs, like I just conferred the greatest
courtesy on him. "Twenty minutes. And Flannery?"

"Yes," I says.

"Don't touch anything."

I go back to the bedroom thinking that one over. Squertsky hands me the death certificate he's just filled out.

"Heart. Wore out. Finally."

He turns to Mrs. Thimble.

"Are you all right?" he asks.

She tears up the way people do when they're feeling fragile but think they got things under control until somebody asks them are they feeling all right. If you left them alone to deal with the crisis in their own way, they probably wouldn't cry, but if you ask them are they all right, it's like they got to show you they ain't all right even if they say they are.

"Go to your room and I'll bring you a little something to make you feel better," he says.

She allows herself to be led to the door with his hand on her shoulder.

He turns to me and says, "I'll give her a mild sedative and then I'll let myself out, Flannery. Is there anything you want?"

"I'm all right," I says, and feel tears welling up in my own eyes.

"He's had a long journey," Squertsky said, looking at Delvin.

"But you know what they say," I says.

"What's that?"

"There's no man so old he don't want another day."

"Health and comfort permitting," Squertsky fires back, letting me know how foolish most such sayings really are.

3

It ain't twenty minutes before Cleary and Diversey arrive. It's more like an hour. I spend the time reading the rest of the instructions Delvin left for me in my capacity as executor trustee.

He's a man what kept his affairs up to date.

He's had the house appraised every two years. The last one, six months ago, values the house at a hundred thousand dollars.

I know most of the furniture he's got and none of it's what you'd call valuable antiques. I figure all of it couldn't be worth more than ten thousand, the most, if it was sold at auction.

Maybe I'm sounding like some sort of ghoul putting a price on what this old friend of mine left me, but it ain't that. I think maybe these chores you're left to do after somebody near and dear to you dies you do more carefully than most, paying attention to every detail, because it gives you a lot to occupy your mind while the grief settles in without busting you apart.

Anyway, it's all there in separate folders, receipts for big pieces bought all the way back in 1936 and '37, when Delvin was a young man just married and setting up house-keeping. He didn't get a television set until 1962. There's a receipt for a new mattress he bought in 1975, which is, I think, right after his wife died.

The instructions point me to folders which contain municipal bonds and zero-coupon federal securities with staggered dates of maturity and two single-premium annuities. He's got some preferred utility stocks and three savings account passbooks plus the active checking account used for everyday expenses.

After I do a quick running calculation in my head, it all adds up to about two hundred thousand dollars, which may not be a fortune to some people but which looks substantial to me. All told, everything in the pot, it's well under the estate tax exemption of six hundred thousand dollars, which is apparently all the federal government figures you should have in your pocket when the trumpets call you home. After that, they want theirs, unless you're so rich that you can afford a team of lawyers and accountants to show you ways to duck.

There's five pages of personal bequests. Little things. Personal mementos.

His pocket watch (which it turns out don't run and can't be fixed) to Wally Dunleavy, which I wonder if it ain't a wry remark, Dunleavy being older than Delvin by somewhat. So if he's still alive when Delvin dies, he'll be getting a watch what can't count the minutes he's got left, which won't be many. It's the kind of thing Delvin would do.

A Phi Beta Kappa key (who knew he'd ever had such an education?) to Janet Canarias, the lipstick lesbian what took the Twenty-seventh away from the party when she ran for alderman the time I refused to run at their request. It turns out that it's the real Phi Beta Kappa key, but it wasn't really his. He never made it past the eighth grade. He probably bought it for hisself in some pawnshop, a token of how good he thought he was or maybe another wry remark about how the honors society hand outs don't always count for much when the chips're down. He kept the receipt for it, so he wasn't trying to fool anybody that he really earned it the old-fashioned way, by going to school. It also showed how much he thought about higher education, you could buy its prizes for thirty bucks.

He leaves a leather photo album to the Chicago Historical Society. It's filled with photographs they'd be glad to get, going all the way back to when part of present-day Bridgeport was called Ducktown because it was flooded so much. Pictures of immigrant Irish and Germans at political picnics, men in bowlers and women in their Sunday bonnets.

Looking at them I get the melancholy feeling I always get looking at old photographs, thinking how all these smiling people squinting in the sun are nothing but dust and bones buried in some old cemetery or maybe sleeping under the asphalt apron of a gas station or a parking lot.

He left a special book to this one and a pair of gold cuff links to that one.

A tortoiseshell spectacle case patched with a sliver of celluloid to my old man.

A gold belt buckle to Ollie Tchinooski, who adjusts the furnace valves, under the supervision of Kippy Kerner, down at the county building, which Ollie don't need because he always wears suspenders to hold up his baggy pants. I never see him wear a belt.

A silver money clip to Polly Lubelski, the warlord of the Twelfth.

In fact there's a little something for all the committeemen and aldermen that've been around for more than ten years. He's had dealings with them all.

There's an old tiepin called a Lover's Knot with a tiny diamond in the center which he wants me to give to Mayor Daley, the sitting mayor, the son of Hizzoner, the mayor of legend. Who wears stickpins any more? But it's a connection to the sweet days of youth and something I know the mayor's going to cherish.

All these things passed out to old friends and acquaintances. All of them described with great care and in great detail in Delvin's last will and testament.

And here I am, the one who's going to get a special benefit from all these gifts, because Delvin was a politician and I'm a politician, and when I deliver these two or three hundred items I'm going to be touching Delvin's entire power base as well as everyone he ever had a kind and tender thought about.

He knows and I understand that it'll mean these people'll have a good feeling about me the next time I bump into them or go to them for some help about this or that. I'll be the beneficiary of Delvin's thoughtful manipulation of favor for favor.

Mrs. Thimble's still in her room when Diversey hisself and his father-in-law, Delvin's old friend, Detective 3, Lou Cleary, Homicide, retired, finally arrive and I let them in.

"Ah, Jesus, Mary and Joseph, it's good to see you again, Jimmy," Cleary says, giving me a big bear hug like a father and son reunited after many years. "You never do get to see enough of the friends you love best, ain't it so?" he went on.

"And it's good to see you, too, Lou."

"I wish it was under better circumstances. You know my son-in-law, Jack Diversey?"

"I've had the pleasure many times," I says, taking the white, pudgy hand which Diversey sticks out at me. "How are you keeping, Jack?"

"Very well, Jimmy," he says, finally letting go of my hand and putting on a pair of surgical gloves, proving to one and all just how fastidious he is when handling the dear departed and also taking no chances what with the infectious diseases that're making a comeback. Not to mention AIDS.

"If you would be so kind as to point the way," he says.

I lead the way down the hall toward Delvin's bedroom, Cleary making small noises with his mouth all the way, comments on the photographs of Delvin's youth and salad days displayed in frames along the walls.

"Here's me at the grand picnic the Sons of Hibernia had in 1956," he says. "There's old Chips on Deke Sullivan's wedding day," he says.

I stop at the door to the bedroom to let them past, Diversey first, then Cleary, who's put on gloves as well. He stands there with his hands clasped in front of his vest, shaking his head gently from side to side.

"Well, he had a good journey," he says.

"Maybe a little lonely the last few years," I says, thinking of Delvin's gradual loss of vigor and political power as the city changed.

"Not too lonely," he says.

I'm wondering what that means when Diversey says, "Lou, would you go out and bring in the basket?"

"Could you do the favor for me, sonny?" Cleary says, putting his hand on his back just above the kidney, indicating that he's having a bit of a pain there.

Diversey hesitates half a tick, like he's about to argue the point, because after all he's the owner of the funeral home and Cleary's boss so to speak, but then he nods and grins and accepts the ruling, as it were. It may be that Cleary's working part-time in his son-in-law's business but he's the kind of man would be the boss most places he happened to find hisself. Diversey hustles out to bring back the empty basket, which they should've brought it with them in the first place.

"So, Jimmy," Cleary croons at me, Irish honey cake spilling from his mouth, "I never had a chance to congratulate you on taking over the ward when Delvin named you warlord. That old devil, there, held on to the job as long as he could, didn't he?"

"Nobody likes to admit they're growing old," I says.

"And why is that, I wonder?" Cleary says. "I find growing old like sailing into a safe harbor, all the trials and tribulations of youth behind me, all the good times living in my heart as rosy memories. Even a lot of the bad things softened by the gentle hand of time."

Oh, oh, I'm thinking, what's he going on about?

"As long as a man's not lonely, you may be right," I says, giving him a chance at another bite of the apple.

"Not that a man ain't better off if he's found some occupation after retirement and if he's lucky enough to be living in the bosom of a loving family. Which, I understand, old Delvin did not. Except for you, Jimmy. He thought about you like you were the son he never had. He had friends, though. Many friends."

"He did," I says, remarking to myself that Cleary's hitting a very long ball here, which means he's trying to figure the right way to bring up whatever it is he wants to talk to me about and wants me looking at the floater while he makes up his mind.

"Loneliness ain't something cannot be avoided altogether, depending on a person's nature," he says, "but I can assure you, Jimmy, old Chips was not lonely when he didn't want to be lonely."

"Well, he did have Mrs. Thimble to talk to," I says.

"I was thinking of female companionship a bit younger and livelier than Mrs. Thimble," he says.

He's staring at me with his head cocked just a little bit, asking the question. Do I understand what is being said here or am I one of them that needs everything spelled out? An old politician's attitude, cop's attitude, cutting deals without saying anything that can later be used as testimony in a court of law or anywhere else.

"Well, I meant lonely those last hours," I says.

"Put your heart to rest. He died happy," Cleary says.

There is a light tapping on the window on the other side of the room. Cleary goes to the drapes and draws them aside, revealing French doors, which I never even knew was there, leading out into the backyard.

Diversey's standing there hold a long, old-fashioned undertaker's wicker basket by one handle.

Cleary opens the doors and gives his son-in-law a hand with the basket. They take the lid off and lean it against the dresser. They lay the open basket on the floor next to the bed. They pull back the covers. Delvin's wearing white socks and a nightshirt, which pokes up above the bottom of his belly like a tent pole.

"Well, God bless the old boy," Cleary says, and looks at me as though he's asking me do I understand better what he meant about Delvin dying happy.

Then he goes to Delvin's head, the heaviest end, and Diversey goes to the feet. They slide the body to the edge of the bed. Cleary puts his hands under Delvin's shoulders and Diversey grabs the ankles and they lift him off the bed and put him down in the basket without a grunt or word of complaint about a sore back from Cleary.

They put the lid back on, pick up the basket, with Delvin in it, and walk it out the French doors, with me following them across the backyard, down the alley and out to their station wagon.

Cleary steps up on the sidewalk to stand beside me as Diversey closes the doors and then goes around front to get behind the wheel.

"You go back in there and check the bedclothes, Jimmy. If you find a smudge of lipstick on the pillow or a hairpin in the bed, you'll know for sure that old Chips was not alone."

"I've never been much for pussyfooting," I says. "Are you by way of telling me that Delvin was entertaining a lady in his bedroom last night?"

"That's a strong possibility," he says.

"But Dr. Squertsky says he had a heart attack."

"I'm sure that's medically correct," Cleary says.

He's peeling off his gloves and putting them in his pocket. He reaches out his hand and I shake it. It's slightly damp.

"He'll be ready for viewing tomorrow afternoon," Cleary says. "Did he have any relatives I don't know about? I seem to remember a cousin."

"An imposter," I says.

"So there's no one to sit the night?"

"I'll sit the night," I says.

"I'll sit tonight and you can sit tomorrow night and the one after that," Cleary says, "and we'll have the burial on Friday morning, not too early. Is that all right?"

I said it seemed fine to me.

"Do you think Mrs. Thimble is up to serving the funeral feast? If not, we can arrange to cater it here at home or at a facility of your choice. The room above Schaller's Pump might be appropriate."

"I think we'll have the feast here at home. My Mary will help Mrs. Thimble and I'm sure neighbors and friends will provide all the food that'll be needed."

"The old way."

"We'll do it right, Lou. Don't you worry."

"Will you need help picking out a suit and shirt and tie?"

"I can do it. What about shoes?"

"Socks but no shoes. I believe in sending a man off in comfort."

Diversey taps the horn, telling me and his father-in-law that he's a busy man and we shouldn't be abusing his generosity seeing as how he come to pick up Delvin hisself out of respect for all concerned.

Cleary nods and says, "And by the way, Jimmy, don't sell yourself short. You're one of the best pussyfooters in town."

4

I go back in the house and sit in the parlor again with the mahogany box on the floor at my feet, going through the rest of the instructions page by page and item by item.

Mrs. Thimble comes out of her bedroom. I can hear her quietly rattling around in the kitchen and after a little while she comes in with a tray in which there's a pot of tea, two cups and saucers, milk and sugar and some wedges of lemon. She sets it down on the coffee table and asks me should she pour.

I ain't really in the mood but I know that this is an important ritual to her. A way of getting a handle on reality.

"Mrs. Thimble," I says, taking the cup from her hand, "would you like to know what arrangements Mr. Delvin made for you?"

"I never expected any arrangement," she says, "except maybe a small token of his regard."

"Well, his regard for you was very great. Very great, indeed. He's formed a trust fund of eighty thousand dollars and made a tentative contract with the Larkspur Retirement Home, which used to be the Larkspur Nursing Home—"

"He told me all about that place," she says, interrupting me.

"Then I guess he also told you that after that trouble we had with them back when he was put in there and after they reorganized and changed their name, they're now considered one of the best facilities in the state."

"He was proud of his part in that."

"The interest on the trust fund and whatever part of the principal it takes to adjust for inflation is to go to your care over there."

She tears up and out comes a little lace-edged hankie, which she presses to her nose.

"And what if I don't choose to go to a convalescent home?"

"Retirement home."

"Whatever they want to call it."

"Then you're to receive forty thousand dollars in cash."

"What about the other forty thousand?"

"That's to be added proportionately to the bequests he made to certain charities."

"Which might they be?" she asks.

"Our Lady of the Sorrow Roman Catholic Church, the Sons of Hibernia Roger Toole Lodge, the Quaker Hospice and the Chicago General Geriatric Ward," I says, she nodding after each one I name as though she approves, though I got to admit she hesitates a little over the Hibernia Lodge, which I have often heard her condemn as a place where old men drink too much.

"I'd rather have the forty," she says. "I can start collecting my Social Security and no matter where I worked, I've always been able to put away practically my whole paycheck. Father Mulrooney . . . God rest his soul . . . remembered me in his will, little as he had, taking the vow of poverty and all. So I have a little invested in IRAs and Keoghs and so forth. I expect I can get a six and a half percent return on the forty thousand in a nice conservative preferred stock, which should amount to twenty-six hundred dollars . . . give or take . . . and that should be enough to pay for a trip to Houston once a year."

I'm sitting there listening to this old lady talking like a stockbroker or a financial planner. She's doing these calculations in her head and I got no doubt that she was so good watching the household money Father Mulrooney and Delvin give her that she saved a little of that, too, figuring a penny saved was her penny earned.

"My cousin Janet lives down there on a cow ranch with her husband, Bob Wilson, and their dog, Rupert," she says. "It's a shar-pei. You know? One of them dogs that looks like a bath towel somebody's thrown on the floor. Apricot color, it is."

She rattles on, and I can tell she's talking about money and these trips to Texas she'll be taking because she don't want to think about the old man they just carried away in a wicker basket.

Also I'm remembering that when I first met her, when she was Father Mulrooney's housekeeper, I learned all about how she came from Nappanee, Indiana, when she was a young woman, and how she killed her husband in self-defense, and how she had no friends or relatives until Father Mulrooney and two other priests took her into the priest's house as housekeeper. So this cousin in Texas is just another example of how people, when they want or need something, alter the truth to make a case. Though they might not have been so friendly back then or the cousin not in any position to offer much help.

"That's what we'll do, then," I says.

"One thing, though," she goes on.

"What's that?"

"I would like to be there when you turn over the checks to them other residual legatees. And if you could just let it drop that I refused the legacy in their favor, I'd be much obliged."

A lot of politicians I know could take lessons from Mrs. Thimble. She refuses a deal which would've forced her to

live where she don't want to live and do what she don't
want to do, but she's smart enough to work it so the forty
thousand she won't be getting by refusing the arrangement
ain't a total loss. If she can work it so her name appears
somewhere attached to these gifts she'll have added to her
bank account in heaven, and assured herself better than average treatment should she ever have to go to any of these
facilities for care. Like if she needs anything the hospice
can provide when her own end of the day rolls around, for
instance. Then, she figures, her generosity may be remembered and she'll be jumped to the head of the line, whatever
that line might be.

You live your life in Chicago, you learn how to take care
of yourself.

5

When I get home, Kathleen's down for her nap. Alfie, who used to be my dog, then became Mary's dog, and is now, definitely, Kathleen's dog, is sleeping at her feet. He doesn't even open an eye when I go in to see that everything's all right.

Mary's napping on the couch in the living room, but she wakes up the minute I kiss her on the cheek. It makes me glad to know she feels secure enough to sleep through me opening the door, putting my key in the lock. Part of that's because we live up on the third floor and not a lot of thieves and house invaders climb up six flights to rob a house in a modest neighborhood like ours. Also Alfie would be up and at 'em, he hears anything out of the ordinary.

Still and all a house, even a house in Bridgeport, is going to be a new way of life, with its own upsides and downsides but mostly up.

I put Delvin's old briefcase, filled with all the papers I scanned, but which I got to read again more carefully, by the side of my chair and I guess Mary hears that because she says, "You all right, James?"

I turn around and look at her, looking up at me like I was

another kid what might have a fever. I kneel down on the rug and put my face closer to hers.

"You look all wrung out," she says, laying her hand alongside my face.

"Ah, no, I'm okay," I says.

"And how about Mrs. Thimble?"

"She's been expecting it. At his age."

"Even so."

"She's got herself set up pretty good for her old age," I says. "People surprise me. You think some people, being sheltered from the real world and all, are helpless when it comes to facing it alone, but she's anything but helpless. She turned down a free ride in a retirement home for forty thousand dollars in cash which she already knows how she's going to invest."

"I'm sure she knows what she's doing. You eat anything today? I can make you something," she says, starting to get up.

"No, no, you stay right where you are. What I could use is a hug right now. So if you'll make me some room on that couch?"

She squinches over with her back against the couch back and I take off my shoes and stretch out next to her.

"Delvin left us his house," I says. "He left us the house and the furniture and enough money to handle the paperwork and the fees and everything."

She's quiet for a long time, taking it in.

"Wow," she finally says.

"Would you mind leaving the neighborhood and moving over to Bridgeport?" I asks.

"Not likely," she says. Then she modifies her enthusiasm, which I think she thinks could hurt my feelings since I'm the one that's always resisted moving out of our building and neighborhood, by saying, "It might be time, James. This isn't the neighborhood it was when you were its precinct captain. I'll bet you don't know half the people in it any more."

She's being generous. I probably don't even know

twenty percent to talk to and maybe not even ten percent on a day-to-day basis.

Sometimes when they come to see me and ask for favors in the ward office, which Janet Canarias, the alderman for the Twenty-seventh, lets me, as the committeeman for the Democratic Party, use on Monday nights and Saturday afternoons, I got to be reminded who they are and where I've met them.

I got to admit, I don't feel so much like I'm doing a favor for a friend and neighbor so much as I'm just another bureaucrat, a little more accessible to them than the ones down to City Hall, but not all that different. Just some gazooney asking them to fill out this form or that piece of paper.

I remember one of the last conversations I had with my old Chinaman before he died.

He says to me, "Jim, you got to accept the fact, the reasons you started doing something ain't the same reasons why you keep on doing it. You liked the idea of helping out your neighbors, ringing doorbells at election time, getting to know everybody and everybody knowing you. But the longer you're at the game the less time you got for putting your foot up on a neighbor's stoop and chewing the fat, even if there's a neighbor sitting out on his stoop of an evening, what with the television, ready to chew the fat with you. You find the people you like get fewer and the people you got to be nice to just to get things done become many."

"You make it sound like there's no way to run your own life," I says.

"What I'm saying is you got to work harder at it if you want things to stay the same because ten million people and events are conspiring to change things. So if you want to climb in your chosen occupation, you got to find the line beyond which you will not go and accept the fact that practically everybody else, after halfheartedly trying to persuade you to stay on the train, will just wave as they go on, leaving you standing on the station platform."

At the time, I wondered if he was regretting chances that maybe he let pass him by, choosing the power he had firmly in his fist over a bigger piece of it that could've slipped through his fingers if he'd reached for it.

After a while I touch Mary on the breast and she moves her hips closer. We make love the way married people with sleeping dogs and children do, slow and quiet, letting all the feelings out in whispers and little moans. And then we sleep.

I ain't sure how long we sleep but the light's changed in the room when we get waked up by Kathleen singing. I got in to get her. She's standing up in her crib, all damp with sleep, grinning at me like I was the bananas.

Alfie lets me know he's happy to see me, too.

Mary gets up to start supper and I go sit in my easy chair with Kathleen on my lap, playing with my fingers. She gets fed up with that after a while and, knowing I'm there and Mary's there and all's right with the world, she crawls down off my lap and goes looking for her favorite teddy bear, a mangy critter that even Alfie knows he's not to touch.

I open up Delvin's briefcase and the other letter to me is on top.

It's a personal letter to me, just like I expected it would be.

Dear Jimmy:

When I used to call you Jimbo it was just to get your goat. I always called you Jimmy in my heart because that's how I would've called my son, if I'd ever had a son.

The rumor out there all these years is that my ability to have children had been ruined by a social disease picked up in my wild youth, but that was never so.

It was my dear wife who couldn't conceive. When we were young there was some tribal shame in that and I saw no reason to let her suffer any humiliation so I let the rumor stand undenied.

I traded favors and gave myself an edge now and then, but I never, stole from the public purse wholesale, nor did I ever deliberately do harm to another human being unless they were sons of bitches who deserved everything I was able to give them by way of retribution for things they done.

There's where the disputes always arise. What a person does, and the reasons he or she might have for doing it, can be easily misunderstood or misinterpreted. So like my father said to me and I often said to you, "Don't complain and don't explain." But here I am explaining, though I'm not complaining.

I've had a good life with some sorrows and sadness . . . don't we all . . . ? but I just wanted you to know that knowing you and watching you learn the ropes has been a bright spot over the years, no matter how often it might have seemed that I was trying to break your legs.

We never really hugged each other, did we? I mean we grabbed hold at picnics, christenings, weddings and funerals, but they were like duty dances. I mean a real hug that lasted more than thirty seconds. My generation didn't do much of that. Your generation does a lot more and I hope the next does more still, because I know now, here at the end, that a loving embrace is one of the nicest things in life.

So here's a hug for you, Jimmy. I love you, laddie.

Mary, coming in to tell me that supper's about to be put on the table, finds me sitting there with tears running down my cheeks. I hand her the letter so she can read it.

"He didn't even sign it," I says. "I guess he wanted to be able to deny it if anybody accused him of having a marshmallow for a heart."

6

They write books about Irish wakes and funerals and people read them and roll on the floor with laughter at the mourners standing the dear departed up in the corner and toasting his good health with glasses of whiskey, the readers thinking it's all ancient history or fairy tales.

Well, I ain't been to any wakes where they expected the corpse to have a drink but I've been to many where there was much singing and drinking and laughter, especially in the old neighborhoods of Chicago where waking the dead in still the custom.

Nowadays most people, most places, don't even lay the body out for viewing. It's in the fire or the ground quick as a wink, like a magic trick, with maybe a memorial service a week or so later, depending how long you got to wait for a caterer.

I ain't a morbid person but I got to say funeral homes don't bother me, not at all. I get the comforting feeling that here's a lot of people taking care of a person I knew, most I liked, some I loved, for the last time, seeing they get sent off with some respect and dignity and even a little joy.

It's true, like everything else, some of the people in the business has gone too far, what with drive-up viewing windows at the curb, powder-blue graduation dresses and tuxedos on aged corpses and other such extravagances that make you want to laugh if you ain't crying while reaching into your pocket to pay for it all.

That ain't the way things is at Diversey's, which is an old-fashioned family-type operation, the sleeping rooms very tasteful, even a little plain, and the extras kept to a minimum.

Oh, Diversey might try to sell you a special set of rosary beads to wrap around the dear departed's hands and pluck the purse strings with a line of special thank-you cards for them what sent flowers, but that's all pretty ordinary stuff.

Maybe it's just that I been to so many wakes and funerals that they truly do feel like social events to me.

Like my Great-Aunt Molly. She used to go to every funeral in the Fourteenth Ward, and a couple in the adjoining wards, where anybody with the name Flannery, O'Connell, Ryan or Hennessy was being put to rest. Which kept her very busy.

Once, she went to the funeral of a Flannery who turned out to be black, but she sat right down and wept through the service, telling my father afterward that black, white, brown or yellow, anyone with the name Flannery, no matter how acquired, was Irish and that's all she needed to know. Not that she didn't go to the funerals of the Giovinnes, Kopchas and Wyzsinskis. She had acquired a lot of friends and acquaintances over the years.

They had to lay her out in the cathedral when she went; the parish church wasn't big enough to accommodate all the mourners what came.

So, anyway, sad as the duty may be, I feel like I'm part of something very useful and affectionate when I go over to Diversey Funeral Home with the clothes Delvin's going to be laid out in: a blue serge suit, a white shirt, silk under-wear and socks and the tie he was given as the president of the Sons of Hibernia maybe thirty years ago. Also the sash of office across his chest.

Lou Cleary takes the clothes and asks me, "Do you want to help dress him?"

"I don't think my devotion to the dear departed goes that far, Lou," I says.

"I understand," he says, "but why don't you at least come in and keep me company while I do the honors."

I'm reluctant, but I go back into the preparation room, where Delvin ain't the only one laid out naked with nothing but a sheet over him.

There's also a woman about forty-five, fifty, who was once a very attractive lady.

Cleary lays the clothes down on a tall table alongside Delvin's steel cot and takes off the sheet.

"For God's sake," I says, "can't you do something about that?"

"Sometimes rigor don't leave the penis for a long time. Occasionally the erection don't go away at all. Especially if it was chemically induced."

"You're making me nervous, here, Lou. Are you saying my old Chinaman, Delvin, was a consumer of illegal sub-stances?"

"I don't mean cocaine or heroin or nothing like that. What I'm talking about here is the self-administered injec-tion of a drug that induces erection in men suffering impo-tence for one reason or another."

"Like advancing age?"

"That could be a reason."

"Are you telling me Delvin gave hisself an injection in the pecker last night before he died?"

"Well, I don't think he got such a wonder simply lusting after the lady laying next to him, even if she was a profes-sional with some special knowledge of such equipment fail-ure."

"I appreciate your black humor, Lou. I suppose you've indulged in a lot of it over the years, considering the professions in which you chose to spend your life, but I got to protest here."

"About what? I'm not making fun. I'm simply saying that a couple of hours before he died, Chips Delvin had reason to help a failing member along in accomplishing a much-to-be-desired act of . . ."

He stops, considering his next words carefully.

"Was you going to say love?" I asks.

"Well, we could have a philosophical discussion about that, if you want."

"I don't think now's the time."

"I agree. Enough to say he had a willing companion of the female gender in his bed and from all that I can ascertain he went out happy or as happy as a man can be who has to stick a needle in his pecker in order to do the necessary."

While we're having this conversation, Cleary's taping the offending member to Delvin's thigh with a roll of cellutape and now he's ready to dress Delvin's bottom half in the silk shorts I brung . . . which is a nice shade of red.

"How do you know so much about these things, Lou?" I asks.

"Well, I ain't had to have recourse to the needle yet, thank God, but I have had many occasions to refer a friend or acquaintance to this very legitimate physician who specializes in such dysfunctions."

"Why would you be making such referrals?" I asks.

"Because working Vice like I did all those years, friends and neighbors look to me as something of an expert, for one thing."

"How about for another thing?"

"Because I believe in full service in any enterprise to which I lend my hand," Cleary says, and then, without missing a beat, asks me, "Would you help me sit him up? I know it can't be seen but I think an undershirt proper attire for a man his age."

"An undershirt but no shoes?" I says, a little irked that here he's got me doing something I said I didn't want to do.

"I know I shouldn't bring my personal preferences into my work but in this case I don't see how it could do any harm."

"Speaking of personal preferences," I says, "where did Delvin satisfy his preference for feminine companionship and how come you know so much about his last night on earth? I get the feeling you ain't just supposing."

"That's what I'd like to talk to you about, Jimmy," Cleary says, buttoning Delvin's white shirt while I'm holding Delvin up with a hand on his back.

"Chips handed you the committeeman's job and he wanted to hand you the Sewer Department as well, I can tell you that, even though it wasn't in his power to do so. Also he was hoping that you'd run for alderman of this ward after you moved your place of domicile. He was always sorry he'd never tried for the job instead of representing the Twenty-seventh, where he kept his accommodation address. Also he wanted you to have a hand in certain enterprises in which he was engaged as a silent partner, more or less."

"Partner?" -

"Bad choice of words, there. More like a facilitator. You know all about facilitating, don't you, Jimmy?"

"If you mean helping the people in my ward, I know a little, but, though I might pick the lock to a door that refuses to open, I won't go breaking in. If you know what I mean."

"I know exactly what you mean, and I'm not asking you to do anything criminal. I'm not asking for an illegal favor but merely for a little of your good counsel and influence for which I would be most grateful."

"I wish the hell you'd tell me just what you want, Lou."

He's got the tie and jacket on Delvin. There's only the trousers and socks to do.

"You can lay him back down," Cleary says.

I lay Delvin back down.

"I was the party what provided Chips with his last bit of joy, if not ecstasy."

"I already figured out you was the one provided the girl but I wanted to hear you say it," I says.

One of the very tricky things about doing favors or asking for favors done is the way you get asked or do the asking. You got to reveal enough to get the job done, of course, but you don't want to tell the other party too much in case they have to deny all knowledge under oath up there in court. You got to understand that there's a lot of people will rob and steal and break somebody's arms and legs, but refuse to lie under oath. Don't ask me why.

So everybody talks sideways so they'll have this privilege of denial. Sometimes it cause difficulties and the wrong person gets the broken arms and legs . . . in a manner of speaking. Which is why I did a dance with Cleary until he comes right out and admits that he supplied the girl.

"Woman," Cleary says. "A very lovely, mature woman a man would be proud to take home to meet his mother. Who'd be proud to *have* as his mother."

"This sweetheart got a name?"

"Fay Wray."

"Wasn't she the girl King Kong fell in love with?"

"I hope you ain't reaching for a metaphor here," Cleary says.

"No, I just remember seeing the picture in that movie house what shows old flicks just off State Street down by the Loop."

"I didn't know you was a film historian," Cleary says, which is his clumsy way of buttering me up.

"I take it that's not the lady's real name," I says.

"She'd prefer to be anonymous. In fact all my female associates in this enterprise prefer to work under professional names. Because many of them, you see, live conventionally respectable lives. I ain't talking floozies or two-bit bints here. I'm talking secretaries, housewives and even a couple of professional . . . I mean like lawyers and accountants professional . . . women doing a little moonlighting to pay for their Cadillacs and Porsches or whatever."

"How long you been in the trade?" I asks.

Cleary winces like I said something what offended him.

"I've been doing this service for friends in City Hall for several years."

"Was you in it while you was a detective?"

"What I done then was only favor for favor and not for money. Since retirement I must admit I've amended that somewhat. But not for Delvin. That was still gratuitous, for free."

"You mean still favor for favor."

"Delvin always told me how you was a stickler for accuracy."

He's struggling to get Delvin's pants on, but I don't move to help and he don't ask me to.

"Delvin's value to me was more symbolic than real," he says.

"A club with which you could threaten competition?"

"He also told me how quick you was."

"I'm quick enough to get out of the way if you was to ask me to front a pimping operation."

"I would never do such a thing. Why don't you ask me what I would like to ask you to do?"

"What would you like to ask me to do?"

"First I got to know your feelings about love for sale."

"You mean prostitution?"

"In the most benign of its many manifestations."

"Well, I ain't no ideologue . . ." I says, using a word which I learned from the book *One Hundred Days to a Stronger Vocabulary* in one of the night school classes I still attend. I was ready to qualify that statement right away but Cleary interrupts me with a "Jesus, Mary and Joseph," in surprise and admiration for my use of the word having trumped his "manifestations" in a single stroke.

I ignore his demonstration of astonishment and go on.

". . . but, like practically everything else I can think of, it all depends on the individual circumstance."

"Like give me a for instance."

"For instance it's all very well and good for people to say it's wrong for a woman to sell her body to pay the rent or put bread on the table for her kiddies and then offer her a job that pays four bucks an hour when rent on a one-room rat farm is two hundred a month. It's something else if she's doing it to feed a drug habit what's going to kill her sooner than later."

"How about a housewife wants a little spice in her life and some extra pin money? How about a college student who works a little bit, in selected situations, until she gets her degree?"

"On the one hand I don't know if it's anybody's business what two consenting adults do in the privacy of their own bedroom or even a hotel room. On the other hand I ain't ready to go along with the notion that prostitution is altogether a victimless crime."

"Well, I see you got a handle on the situation, Jimmy," Cleary interrupts, clearly not really wanting to get into a full-scale debate on the subject, only wanting to establish in his own mind that I had reasonable doubt about what was unacceptable sinning. "At least you give it some thought. But for the sake of brevity let me give you a particular situation drawn from my own extensive experience, which, you got to admit, is probably greater than yours.

"Say you got a woman of mature years. Maybe a divorced lady or a widow. Kids grown or maybe she never had any kids. This lady is brainy, she's got an education and she's kept herself in fine shape. But she puts herself out there and what is she offered in the job market?"

"Minimum wage?" I says, holding up my end of the conversation.

"Maybe a little better if she's got some marketable skills, but not a helluva lot better. So she meets a nice man in this neighborhood cocktail lounge where she occasionally stops in for a recreational drink to hold off the loneliness for an hour or two."

"Is this really a nice man?" I asks.

"The nicest, except he's married."

"Uh-huh."

"But a good man. Good husband and good father. Except the kids is grown and he's feeling a little redundant so far as doing for them is concerned. Except the body he's laying in bed with he's been laying in bed with for thirty years. Except he's hit the wall so far as his job is concerned. No hope for glory here. And he's lost his interest in baseball ever since the strike."

"So what we got is a hungry man on the prowl," I says.

"Is what we got," Cleary agrees. "So he starts off buying our lady friend a couple drinks. Then a dinner. Then he walks her home."

"You don't got to take me all the way into her bedroom," I says.

"You got the picture?"

"I got the picture."

"When the landlord bumps the rent on her, this fellow picks up the slack. Also he buys her gifts. A new dress here, half a dozen pairs of stockings there. Not paying for what he's getting, you understand, just doing what he thinks is right."

"He don't want to admit that he's buying her services is what you're saying."

"Exactly. Then he drops dead of a heart attack."

"Not while amorously engaged, I hope," thinking that Delvin ain't the first and only client to keel over while in the arms of one of Cleary's angels of mercy, which a fan of black humor might call angels of death.

"While on his way to Evanston to see his old mother in a nursing home there," Cleary says, bringing me down to earth.

"I understand the tragedy here," I says. "We got a grieving mother, a grieving wife and I don't know how many children—"

"Three."

"—grieving plus we got a mistress—"

"Lady friend."

"—what the family don't even know about, also devastated by this loss."

"Over and above the personal grief, we got practical considerations."

"She's lost her paycheck."

"I wish you wouldn't put it that way. For the purposes of this illustration let's call it fringe benefits: the little extras this loving friend provided."

"So she figures she did it once, why not try to find another nice man."

"Which, as any decent woman will tell you, ain't so easy to find. Oh, she knows a couple of fellows from the cocktail lounge but they ain't interested in a relationship like the first one was. A little party now and then, maybe, but nothing permanent and nothing too costly."

"So she accommodates them when she runs short at the end of the month."

"Right. Now, you know what they say about easy money."

"It's hard to turn your back on it once you tasted it."

"In a manner of speaking. So her activities become a little more regular and her business methods a little more obvious."

"Until she gets picked up by undercover Vice."

"A man with a heart, who don't want to put this respectable lady in the system. You understand what I'm saying here?"

"You're telling me how this anonymous lady got into the life and how this anonymous cop became a procurer."

"Since we're dealing with hypotheticals, let's call it that, if you got to call it something."

"It's better than pimp."

"We ain't getting judgmental here, are we?" Cleary says.

I apologize because that's exactly what I'm doing and I should know better.

One of the big lessons I learned in life is that everything lays out on a scale of gradations. What you might call a spectrum. Now, you walk along that spectrum and one person says they've gone from white to gray in one spot and somebody else says they crossed the line somewhere else.

There's not a reason in the world for me not to believe that Cleary started out being softhearted about a decent woman fallen on hard times. So maybe he took a little comfort, pleasure or entertainment from her hisself, as a favor returned for not putting her in jail.

Then down the road some friend or ranking associate expresses the desire to provide a couple of girls for the bachelor party he's organizing for a friend. Cleary calls up the lady and she and a couple of girlfriends does the job. There's a fifty in it for Cleary, who can use the extra change. And like that, he's in business.

"Is this hypothetical housewife, who was the first of the ladies this hypothetical vice cop took under his wing, the same hypothetical lady who gives our old friend, Delvin, the last pleasure-filled hour of his life?" I asks.

"Well, no. Time marches on, as you well know, Jimmy, and this would be another lady altogether."

So what we've got here is that by and by Cleary's running a string. When he retires, the extra money ain't just extra. What with rising prices, even the part-time at his son-in-law's funeral home ain't enough to make ends meet, so he figures there's no reason for him not to put this sideline on a regular-paying basis.

You don't have to be a rocket scientist to figure out that

Delvin was his political protection and now that he's dead Cleary has to look elsewhere. Also his business is being threatened or he wouldn't be coming after me so soon. He could wait on it until the grieving for the old man was over a decent length of time.

"I can't give you a general yes to whatever it is you want me to do, Lou. I hope you understand that. All I can do is take things in pieces, a step at a time, on a case-by-case basis, until and if I come up against something I can't go along with. Tell me. What's your immediate problem?"

"Unfair competition."

"Somebody moving in on you?"

"Seeing a target of opportunity now that old Delvin's gone."

"Is this somebody mob-connected?"

"A singleton out there wanting to expand."

"Using muscle and threat of injury?"

"Worse."

"What could be worse?"

"This gazooney's offering the ladies health insurance and a retirement package guaranteed by an annuity."

"And what is it you want me to do?"

"Just have a friendly talk with her and tell her to take her modern management methods elsewhere."

"Her? Your competition is a lady?"

"One way of looking at it."

I think about that a minute and then I say, "I think I can do that. Give me a name and a number."

"Mabel Halstead."

"Mabel Halstead!" I practically yell. "Mabel Halstead what used to be Milton Halstead? Milton Halstead what used to be a cop?"

"You know this Mabel Halstead?"

"She saved my ass from a terrible beating once upon a time."

7

It ain't done much any more. Maybe there's a few old families in which the oldest son or a brother or a father might sit up with the dead the first long night they're laid out.

Cleary says he did the honors for Delvin last night, but I got my doubts. I know all about cops on foot patrol and in the cars finding a place to kip down for fifteen minutes, a half an hour, during a tour. I hear detectives bitch and moan about trying to stay awake on stakeout, drinking so much coffee they're up for hours after they're finally relieved by another team, pissing every half hour.

So I figure Delvin was laying here alone Tuesday night and he'll be laying here alone tomorrow night, the next morning being the burial, but now it's Wednesday midnight and I'm sitting there with a corpse wondering what the hell I'm doing it for.

"To show a little respect, you git," I hear Delvin say, plain as day.

I know something, a sound, a thought, an itch behind my left ear, my senses jogged from a hundred places all at once, got together and started a tape in my head.

Sometimes, when I'm standing on the roof around twilight on a summer's day, with the sounds of the traffic coming up from the streets like the sounds of ocean surf and the smell of fresh-washed sheets hanging on the line, I can close my eyes, and a breeze touches my cheek, and I can hear my mother . . . God rest her soul . . . calling my name.

I look at Delvin laying there, his head on a satin pillow, which would make him sick or mad as hell. That old white head and red face on a satin pillow. We do the damnedest things to the dead. Painting their cheeks and rouging their lips and making them lay their heads on satin pillows.

I remember the first time I met Chips Delvin, sent to his office by a connection my father had from his being a fireman in the Fourteenth, which was old George Lurgan's ward back then.

I was living with my mother and father in a flat in North Park, and my old man set it up with Delvin because he had political ambitions for me . . . which I also had somewhat . . . and he claimed that it would be a smart move. George Lurgan was sure to pass the ward on to his son George Junior, and as it turned out he did and young George ran it for one term before Hilda Moskowitz come along and snatched it way from him.

Anyway, the idea was, Delvin and his wife had no children and there was a strong possibility . . . according to my old man . . . that if Delvin helped me with a job in the Sanitation Department and also in the Democratic Party, he might take a liking to me and I might become his heir. Which came to pass with me being handed the committeeman's job in the Twenty-seventh, though, the party being so much changed and the machine so battered and busted, I wasn't sure I'd been done any big favors at the time.

But I was twenty back then, and it also could've been that he and my mother wanted a little more room to stretch their legs in the little flat we had and it not being such a good thing for me to still be hanging around the nest.

Looking at Delvin's face rising in the coffin off that satin pillow, white hair, hollow cheeks and pinched mouth, I can see him like he was back then, me twenty and him . . . what? . . . maybe sixty-eight. Not a young man by any reckoning but a vigorous man able to take his place at third base in the Fourth of July Picnic softball game over to the Grove.

"Well, Jimbo," he says, giving me the old one-eye, because maybe he knows nobody likes to be called their name with an oh at the end like you're some clown expected to do a tap dance. He wants to see how I'll take it.

"My mother calls me James," I says, "and my father calls me Jim. My pals and most of my friends call me Jimmy. Take your pick, Mr. Delvin."

"But don't call you Jimbo?"

"Well, you can do that, too. How can I stop you?"

So I put it in his lap. He can be an asshole if he wants to keep it up.

"Okay, Jim, what can I do for you?"

"I'm making a move from the Fourteenth to the Twenty-seventh."

"Because you got a girl in East Garfield Park?"

"I like the neighborhood," I says.

At this time I don't know that he lives in the Eleventh even though he's the Democratic committeeman and the alderman from the Twenty-seventh and has the office I'm standing in right there. He's got this accommodation address and he ain't the only one, for one reason or another, decides to run for office in another ward than the one he's living in. It's something like the English do, running for seats known to be safe for their party in Parliament.

"What's your opinion of shit?" he asks, just like that.

"Well, sir," I says, "I'm not going to lie to you and tell you I relish the thought of wading around in rivers of it, but I'm a young man without much education and jobs with a future are not all that easy to find."

"Look at it this way," he says, "it'll teach you humility,

perseverance, tolerance and, once you work your way up out of the sewers, in ten or fifteen years, you'll have the incentive never to do anything that'll put you back in the pipes. How's your politics?"

"I'd say I was a fiscal conservative and a social liberal," I says.

"Which means?"

"Do what you can for the people and bring them the services they need, but make damn sure every penny's spent wisely and you always get the most bang for your buck."

"I want you to understand something, Jimmy," he says, "it ain't the answers to these questions that matter in my decision, it's the way you answer them. If you're feeding me Irish honey cake, I'm not aware of it. You could be lying to me but I think you're sincere about wanting to do good for your neighbors. If you're pulling the wool over my eyes with an act, that's all right, too, because it means you're a good actor and good acting's what a politician needs above all."

He sticks out his hand.

"You've got the jobs," he says.

"Jobs?" I says.

"You start walking the pipes on Monday and you come to ward headquarters on Saturday and we'll show you how to walk the precincts."

He looks down at his desk like there should be some papers that need his attention on it, though there's nothing there, letting me know our business has been completed.

I walk to the door. Then I stop before leaving and ask him one more question.

"Begging your pardon, Mr. Delvin, but did you spend five to fifteen years in the sewers?"

"I never spent a day," he says. "My connection was better than your connection."

8

I never seen such a turnout for a local personality since the old mayor, Richard J., was laid out to receive the city's last respects.

Maybe there ain't as many national politicians stopping by, and even delegations from the state are a little thin on the ground, but at the grass roots, among the foot soldiers of the party, which may be bruised and battered but ain't dead yet, you never seen so many people.

I ain't going to name them all, it could take forever, except to say that Vito Vellitri, alderman and warlord of the Twenty-fifth, a vigorous man in his late sixties who looks as fragile as a piece of porcelain; Carmine DiBella, the mob boss, who naturally springs to mind when you think of Vellitri, him being the one Italian in Chicago DiBella can't intimidate; Big Ed Lubelski, committeeman from the Thirty-second; Ed Keady, the same from the Forty-seventh and also Park District supervisor; Janet Canarias, the Puerto Rican lipstick lesbian, who's alderman in the Twenty-seventh, where I'm the new warlord since old Delvin handed it to me not long before his death; and Wilson Frost, the black leader of the Thirty-fourth, was all there.

Also Hilda Moskowitz is there representing the Fourteenth, sitting right next to George Lurgan, who once held the seat, having been handed it by the party after his father's death. They're chatting away like they don't mistrust one another like a cat mistrusts a dog.

Police Superintendent Smith Jarwolski arrives in full uniform, just to honor old Chips.

Captain Pescaro and the two cops I know best, O'Shea, the rough, and Rourke, the smooth, come in and sit down quietly in the back of the room on two folding chairs hardly strong enough to support such big men.

Hackman the medical examiner and Brigid Monahan the ex-nun, now the public defender, are just a few of them what represents the rest of the police and legal establishment.

We got Hicky Isadore from the Board of Education; Willa Washington from the Health Department; Jack Reddy, the Water Department superintendent; Ray Carrigan, Democratic Party leader; and Wally Dunleavy, Streets and Sanitation, looking his age, which is about ninety, for the first time I can remember.

Patrick Carew, archbishop of Chicago, and Monsignor Harrigan, the slick financial adviser for the archdiocese, sweep in, the archbishop looking a little puzzled like he don't know when he's supposed to deliver the eulogy.

But even his entrance gets pushed to the back of everybody's memory when the mayor walks in with his aides and with the man who is probably the most prominent national political figure in town at the moment; Representative Leo Lundatos, Leo the Lion, known as the Prince of the Greeks.

As a proportion of the population the Greeks might not be very large but for some reason nobody ever explained to me, one seat on the Sanitary District Board always goes to a Greek and it's from that seat that Lundatos launches his spectacularly successful political career thirty-five years ago.

As a young man of thirty, after working as a plumber and union organizer, having quit high school at sixteen, he gets appointed to the board and goes to live in the Thirtieth Ward not far from the Sanitary Ship Canal.

From this position of some power and influence he's able to reach out and snatch the committeeman's job and the alderman's chair whenever it suits him, which he does.

I think I mentioned once or twice that maneuvering an ambitious rival into the State Legislature or even the United States Congress is just a way for incumbents to get a pest out of their hair. Such service for state or country is considered a death warrant as far as Chicago politics is concerned.

That's what you call conventional wisdom, but like everything else, it ain't exactly the whole truth. There's always the exception. There's always them what takes the lemons you toss at them and turn them into lemonade.

When a couple of old lions start getting worried about this young cub who's being groomed by the old mayor, and offer him a rump roast, Lundatos surprises them and jumps at the chance to go to Springfield and the State Legislature.

Before he even finishes out the first term, he runs for the United States Congress from his congressional district and there he is, out of everybody's hair like they wanted him to be.

In a maneuver that for a junior congressman leaves everybody dazed and out of breath he ends up on the very powerful Finance Committee and within three years he's the chair.

He lets the old Chicago and Cook County pols know that when he growls it means he's not pleased with how they're running things in Cook County and the city of Chicago, and he's got the ways and means of shutting off some of the sugar that sweetens the federal appropriations they're used to getting for their coffee.

Not only that, but he makes it clear to one and all that

he's in Washington to stay. Although he holds on to his committeeman's job, he lets them know that they'll see him back in Chicago pressing the flesh during a campaign season or when he wants to visit the properties he owns all over town.

For a quarter of a century he's been throwing his weight around pretty good, one of the movers and shakers, but it's the idea he's got in his head that even though he ain't living in Chicago any more he can still conduct his business Chicago style what gets him in trouble.

He gets careless.

Maybe careless ain't exactly the right description. What he does is he commits the cardinal sin of the professional politician. He gets cocky. He gets arrogant. He thinks he's above the rules that run everybody else and since the United States Congress in general has got a whole set of laws and special privileges us ordinary people don't enjoy, the extra cream he pours on his portion of perks makes a dish too rich for even a whole pack of lions to digest.

What he does, Lundatos, Leo the Lion, is he gives friends and relatives silver cigarette boxes and his picture in frames made of rare tropical woods.

He gets several cousins, nieces and nephews jobs in government, a couple of which collect their paychecks but never show up for work. There's one what never even leaves Chicago, though she's down on the books as a personal assistant.

There's some speculation that this personal assistant might be giving Lundatos assistance a lot more personal than ordinary, which might upset the congressional investigators and Republicans what are trying to bring him to his knees, but which the voters from his district don't give a rat's patootie. They think he should have a little company in the lonely nights when he's visiting Chicago, what with his wife back in their house in Georgetown. At least that's the way it used to be before women changed the rules of the game.

Of course, his enemies is conflicted over this matter because some of their own has been accused of playing around with secretaries, assistants, interns and aides, some even underage at the time the transgressions was committed, so the real thrust of the investigation gets back to money, which such investigations usually do.

The worst they got against him, at least the thing what first brings him to the attention of the Congressional Budget Office, is; he takes money out of the office petty cash to buy hisself and some drinking buddies lunches here and there.

It's not so bad during all those years when the Democrats is running the store but when they lose control of Congress to the Republicans in the night of the long knives, election day 1994, the old lion becomes a target. Truth be known, there's plenty of his own pride . . . which is lion talk for gang . . . would just as soon drop him in the stew as not.

"You know what happens to old politicians after they get kicked out of office?" a voice asks me at my shoulder.

I turn to look at who's about to make a joke and see Tony Carlucci grinning at me with his sidekick Brian O'Ryan next to him. They was firemen with my father but didn't take retirement until a couple of years ago, maybe six or seven years after my old man took his.

They used to know everything that was going on in the city and helped me out with information more than once. I got no doubts that retirement or no retirement they still hear plenty because I never see two guys on the eary as much as Carlucci and O'Ryan.

"They become pretzel benders and ventriloquists," O'Ryan says.

"Butt out," Carlucci says, "this is my joke."

"So tell it already," O'Ryan says.

"They become pretzel benders and ventriloquists because all they know how to do is tie themselves in knots dodging questions while talking out of both sides of their mouths."

"That's a joke?" O'Ryan says. "I'd fall down laughing except it ain't polite to laugh too loud at lie-ins."

Carlucci takes no offense.

"How you doing, Jimmy?" Carlucci says. "You staring at the old lion wondering how he made it to the top and then got his paw caught in a trap?"

"You know Lundatos?" I asks.

"From the old days, sure," O'Ryan says.

"You looking for an introduction?" Carlucci asks.

"I got no particular reason to meet the man," I says.

"Well, you're going to meet him if you want to or not, because here he comes and he's got his eye on you."

9

It ain't only Lundatos what looks like he's making a bee-line toward me, it's also the mayor hisself and a half a dozen of his aides and bodyguards.

The mayor, looking so much like his late lamented father, Hizzoner, that it gives me a start, has got his hand out and a big Irish smile on his kisser. I met the man maybe once or twice, except for a passing nod here and there, now and then, this political function and that. I look at the glad hand he's sticking out at me and I know I'm about to be used or asked a favor.

We shake hands.

"Jimmy Flannery, is it?" he says. "Is it too late for me to congratulate you on your appointment as committeeman of Francis Delvin's ward? Do you know the Honorable Leo Lundatos, the distinguished representative to the Congress of the United States?"

"Oops," Lundatos says.

"Late representative, I meant to say," the mayor corrects hisself.

"Oops," Lundatos says.

The mayor looks confused for a second.

"I ain't dead yet," Lundatos says.

"Ex-representative," the mayor says, high color pouring up out of his white collar, flooding his neck and face. He's got the kind of Irish complexion that shows every bit of his feelings and he's giving away the fact that he ain't pleased being corrected the way Lundatos just corrected him, half in fun but half meaning it, too, trying to show the world that he might be in temporary disgrace but he can still make a power like the mayor dance a little jig just to stay on his good side.

It's a cop's trick, a priest's trick, a politician's trick, setting up a game without giving you the rules, beating you at it when you got no idea what's on the table. It looks like a little thing but it ain't so little. It's like executives playing musical telephones to see which one actually picks up the phone to talk to the other one first, letting their secretaries do the old two-step for fifteen minutes until the connection gets made.

"Late representative," says Lundatos, laughing like it's a great joke on him, taking my hand in a paw as big as a dinner plate and as soft as a nun's.

"I can't tell you what a pleasure it is to meet you, Congressman," I says, laying it on with a trowel.

"Try," Lundatos says, and laughs again, shaking this mane of white hair, which is part of the reason why they call him Leo the Lion. "I'm ready to tell you what a pleasure it is to meet you, Mr. Flannery. Can I call you Jim? Call me Leo if you want to. The mayor's been telling me who's this and who's that, and he has nothing but good things to say about you."

The mayor turns away, already reaching out a hand and smiling into another face, but he's nodding in agreement as he turns and I understand that Lundatos just got handed off to me. The mayor's done his duty by a fellow Democrat and now he can get some distance between hisself and this ex-congressman who's still under attack.

He's already drifted off with his bunch of attendants, relieved to have palmed Lundatos off on me.

Lundatos reads my mind.

"If you was an ear of corn, you'd slip right out of my fingers, is that what you're thinking?" Lundatos says.

"The thought flitted across my mind," I says.

"Well, it flitted wrong. I say what I mean and mean what
I say. I didn't need Richard to give me your biography. I've
heard of you more than once, more than twice. I don't go
around buttering somebody up just to keep in practice. Not
like the mayor over there who's putting some distance between him and me, so he shouldn't get splattered if I self-
destruct. I'd like to have a talk with you."

"Well, I'm sort of like the official greeter at this affair," I
says, "Mr. Delvin not having any family, immediate or otherwise."

"They tell me that, too. That you're a man who knows
how to honor the fundamental values to which we all subscribe."

I hope he ain't saying that he thinks I'll subscribe to dipping into the administrative funds provided the ward offices
by the Democratic Central Committee every time I'm short
of pocket change.

"I understand," he says. "This ain't the time or place, but
soon."

Then he's gone, just like the mayor done, his own watch-
ers at his back, working the crowd like he's still running for
office.

The room's getting so crowded on this first evening of
the viewing that I need some fresh air, so I raise an eye-
brow, a recently acquired talent, at my wife, Mary, who's
sitting with some ladies in the first row of honor usually reserved for family. She nods and gives a lift of her own eye-
brow, letting me know she'd like to be catching a breath
with me if she could.

I don't smoke but the porch around the funeral home on
three sides is filled with men, and some women, smoking.

I'm thinking I could get better air inside the slumber room than I can outside, when I spot Janet Canarias standing by the railing all by herself. So I go over there and give her a kiss on the cheek.

"I don't see you over to the neighborhood headquarters," I says, speaking about the office she keeps open in the Twenty-seventh so them what don't like to come downtown to her offices there can make their complaints and requests in familiar surroundings.

"I sometimes wonder what my job is, Jimmy. Am I supposed to spend most of my time listening to people's troubles, getting a shade tree trimmed which is interfering with somebody's morning sun or seeing to it that a minority teenager gets a shot at a city summer job—"

"That's the sort of thing I'm supposed to do for you," I says.

"—or am I supposed to spend most of my time down at City Hall, biting and scratching for a fair share of the pie?"

Then she catches up with my remark, takes my hand and says, "I know you do."

So I know she's just venting, which is this new thing they say about people what are just blowing off steam. Any job where you got to deal with the public can get on your nerves more than somewhat, every now and then.

"We should thank our lucky stars we can concentrate on the people from one ward," she goes on. "What's it like to get elected to a governing body where you're expected to take care of your constituents on the one hand and the greater county, state or national good on the other?"

"You mean like the Honorable Leo Lundatos's been doing for twenty-five years?" I says.

"Well, yes, like that," she says. "I saw you talking to him. Was he working you for something? Is he still playing the game?"

"He wants something but he ain't got around to telling me what, this not being the time and place."

"I'm surprised he played the game so badly at the end."

"Like how?"

"Like giving old pals and new playmates expensive gifts, bronze statues and crystal vases paid for out of the public purse."

"Them things wasn't actually paid for by public funds," I says. "The way I understand it most of it come from the unspent campaign contributions which he could've walked away with in his pocket in he wanted."

"Not if he wanted, Jimmy, not anytime he wanted. Only if he retired before they changed the law."

"Well, he had plenty of time to do just that."

"And Nixon had plenty of time to destroy the tapes and tell the investigators he trashed them because they were his property and none of their damn business. But he wanted to test the executive privilege of the presidency and got his paw caught in the trap."

"Even so, don't you think he's got a little bit of a case there? I mean there's . . . what . . . fifty-five thousand dollars involved here."

"That's just the tab on the doorstops and paperweights. Then there's the ghost employees and dinners out, leased automobiles for personal use and this and that as you like to say. But, you're right, who cares a hundred thousand here and a hundred thousand there, as some people also like to say. You and I both know it's not about money, Jimmy. It's about power and the arrogance of power. These old bulls and bears and lions holding on to their privileges to the bitter end."

"I can't say no to that, Janet," I says. "But it ain't that simple, as you know as good as me or anybody else."

"Amen to that."

"You got troubles on your mind?" I asks.

"I've been getting delegations of neighborhood women coming in. They want the prostitutes off the streets."

"Again?"

"No, still, Jimmy, and don't start shrugging it off like men do."

"I ain't shrugging nothing off," I says. "I just don't know what you can do about it. Read your Bible. It's been going on for a hell of a long while. It's had its ups and downs. Sometimes it was legal, sometimes not. Sometimes it was even considered an honorable career for a woman."

"But nobody's really figured out how to fit it into an orderly society yet," Janet says.

"Are we having a philosophical conversation here?" I asks, smiling at her. "What in particular do they want you to do about it and what are you going to do about it?"

"I'm not sure I can do what they want me to do. I'm not even convinced I should do it."

"What's that?"

"I don't see how I can ask the police to harass these women with sweeps and arrests in sufficient numbers and with sufficient frequency to convince them that they should stop their activities. All they'd do is move them elsewhere."

"But at least they'd be off the streets of our neighborhoods. That's the way your ladies think."

"As they should. But then the aldermen from neighboring wards accuse me of shoving our garbage into their neighborhoods and they'll refuse to cooperate with me on other matters important to me and my constituents when they come before council."

"That's the way it works."

"I'd just like to find a way to get them off the streets."

"I'll think about it," I says.

Just then this person catches my eye walking up the steps of the funeral home. At first I think it's a man because of the short haircut. Plus the white shirt, black tie and black suit. This person's got to be well over six feet tall, with shoulders like a linebacker, even though the cut of the jacket plays them down.

Then I see the jacket ain't cut exactly like a man's jacket, there's a kind of flare to it, and it's got these flamboyant lapels. Also the trousers break over the shoe front to back like a woman's tailored slacks break. So I figure it's a woman and because Janet Canarias is a lipstick lesbian I figure she probably knows her.

"What's that?" I asks.

"You know her, Jimmy," Janet says. "That's Mabel Halstead."

"Milton?"

"Mabel."

"She still work for you?"

"There's not much for her to do in a year when I'm not campaigning and I couldn't afford to keep her on as a paid employee full-time. She still gives me some hours every now and then."

"What employment has she found?"

"I think she set up her own business. Personal security. She has the experience for it. You know she was a cop when she was a he?"

"Well, yes I do. I think I'll just go over there and thank her for coming."

"I think she'd like that," Janet says.

But I get waylaid by some new arrivals on my way over. By the time I break away all I get to see of Mabel is her kneeling on the prayer stool by the casket. As I walk down the aisle to have a word with her, she gets up and slips away out the side door.

10

Friday morning we bury Delvin over to St. Mary's, where his mother and father is buried, not over to old St. Pat's, where his grandmother's buried and which we once saved from the excavators' bulldozers by declaring it a sacred Indian burial ground.

There's maybe two hundred people at the graveside.

Later on almost everybody comes over to Delvin's old house for the funeral feast which Mrs. Thimble, my wife, Mary, my mother-in-law, Charlotte, and Mary's Aunt Sada, and any number of women known to him or in the neighborhood has helped prepare and put on the table in the big dining room.

There's a smell of lemon oil and wax rising above the smells of salad dressings and roasts. I know that Mrs. Thimble has been cleaning the house from top to bottom ever since the morning when Delvin's body was taken away.

It's got everything to do with the old ways, the house having to look its best because strangers'll be coming over, her reputation as a housekeeper on the line, though

Delvin let her do little enough dusting and cleaning when
he was alive.

Among the ladies is a quiet, sweet-faced woman with
flaming-red hair, probably colored, wearing a simple
navy-blue dress with white polka dots and white collar
and cuffs. She stands out because she don't seem to have
much to say to the other women, answering when asked a
question but not volunteering anything on her own.

When I'm going around the table filling my plate, she
works it so I jostle her a little bit like it's by accident.

"I'm sorry," I says.

"Oh, that's all right, no harm done," she murmurs.

"I never seen so many people crowded in one room," I
says.

"Mr. Delvin was a well-loved man," she says.

"Did you know him very good?" I asks.

She hesitates for just a second and then she says,
"Well, yes, I did."

"Relative?"

"Friend."

"I thought I knew every one of his friends," I says.
"But just this minute I realized that they was all his political friends I knew. There's probably a whole lot of people out there he was friendly with what I don't know and
never even met."

By this time I got a full plate and she's got a small
plate, mostly salad, and we've sort of drifted out to the
kitchen, where Mary glances up as I nudge open the
screen door and go out into the side yard, which you
could not call a garden except for some gigantic hydrangea bushes against the fence.

I doubt that Delvin's spent any time sitting at the table
there, where he and his wife may have once taken tea on
a warm summer's evening, since his wife died many
years ago. The hydrangea is a testimony to how a lot of
flowers thrive on neglect once they get established. Like
some people.

There's a couple of painted cast-iron chairs and a table left over from better times. I dust off one of them with my handkerchief and ask the lady, whose name I ain't yet learned, to sit down, which she does with a thank-you and a nod of her head. I sit down in the other chair facing her.

"What did you want to talk to me about?" I says, leaving an expectation at the end of the sentence so she can fill in a name.

"Fay Wray," she says.

I act surprised though I ain't all that surprised.

"You mean like the actress what played in the original *King Kong*?"

"The one who lost her dress when the gorilla picked her up and gave a generation of boys and men night dreams."

I think she's having a little fun with me, testing the waters, being just a little risqué here.

"What do you want to know, Mr. Flannery?" she asks, putting kidding aside and getting right down to brass tacks.

"I beg your pardon."

"You didn't bring me out here for a private picnic," she says, still smiling sweetly.

"Well, you nudged me and I knew you wanted a private chat," I says. "I got to admit I been wondering about you."

"You've been looking around like a hawk trying to figure which one of the many women present was the lady who spent Frank's last hour in bed with him."

"You can understand a person would have a natural curiosity."

"Of course I can. In fact it's a little bit of my stock-in-trade. Natural curiosity. A man brags to a friend about being friendly with me." She hesitates just a tick over the word friendly, putting a spin on it, every other word out of this lady's mouth an innuendo, an invitation to a dance. "The friend grows very curious and, sooner or later, more often than not, I get a phone call."

"So, is coming here like merchandising the product?"

"That wasn't kind, Mr. Flannery, and I'm surprised at you for making a remark like that. I don't sell myself on the hoof."

She's got me dead to rights because what I was doing here was I was reacting to what she was saying about men acting on this curiosity about her and women like her and I wanted her to know I wasn't so inclined. Which she's got every right to resent, since I made a judgment on her. Also since I got defensive, in a manner of speaking, it could be that I entertained such thoughts about some woman more than once or twice. Which what man ain't?

"I came here because I had a deep affection for Frank," she says. "He was a good man. And, from all that he confided in me, a very lonely man, these last several years."

"I'm sorry for the wisecrack."

She accepts my apology with a nod of her head, the forgiveness of a queen.

"He reminded me of my own father very much," she said. "A man of old-fashioned values."

"I understand," I says, and the fact is I do understand.

"Why don't you ask the question, Mr. Flannery?"

"Which one is that?"

"What's a nice lady like me doing in a life like this."

"What's a nice lady like you doing in a life like this?" I says.

"I'm sure Mr. Cleary told you the one about the good mother with the invalid child or the maiden lady schoolteacher fallen on hard times or the newly made widow who discovers that her husband has gambled away their annuities."

"He give me a different one altogether," I says. "He give me the one about the widow and the gentleman in the cocktail lounge."

"They're all much the same."

"Which one are you?" I asks. "If I ain't being too personal."

"I'm the divorced lady, tossed aside for a young body half her age, who wasn't smart enough to fight for her rights. Who hired the wrong lawyers and got the short end of the financial settlement. Who let the house be sold and walked away with the oldest of two cars and a fraction of the assets her husband and herself had accumulated over twenty-five years of marriage."

"Children?"

"No children. Maybe that's part of why I didn't try to fight so hard for what was mine. Shame for being barren. Trying to make up for not giving him children and not wanting to adopt. Maybe I believed him when he said he wanted a chance for a family with this other woman. This young woman with the hard body. Oh, hell." She made a gesture like she was brushing away ghosts or demons. "How retarded can you get?"

I just sat there, nibbling at the potato salad, not wanting to pick up the leg of cold chicken while she was telling me her sad story.

"I wasn't living in a refrigerator carton," she goes on. "I wasn't pushing a shopping cart around. I had a very nice little sublet flat over on the North Side and a job at an upmarket boutique and I drove a little Honda. And then the you-know-what hit the fan."

"You lost your job?"

"No, I even got a promotion and a small raise in salary. But Harry, my ex, lost his job in middle management. He was too far back in the stick when they kicked him out of the plane and he wasn't given a golden parachute. Then his little wife ran off with a foreign motor mechanic . . . that is, a mechanic who repaired foreign cars . . . and whatever money she hadn't already spent, leaving him with enough credit card debt to bring a mule to its knees."

I'm wondering if I'm being worked a little bit here, though she's got no reason to sing any sad songs for me. The way she tells the story and the way she don't check me out with little glances to see how it's selling convinces me that what I'm hearing is the truth, even if it ain't the whole truth and nothing but the truth, which is more than anybody can expect of anybody, even somebody you know for a hundred years.

"Eat your chicken," she says, like she knows I want a bite.

"So, what then?" I says, taking a nibble. "What decided you to start moonlighting at another trade?"

"Harry begged me for another chance, claiming everything including temporary insanity. But I wouldn't have it. I was enjoying his suffering too much. Also I didn't trust him. That's always the worst of infidelity. It isn't difficult to forgive the sin and embrace the sinner . . . except you know the old saying?"

"Fool me once, shame on you. Fool me twice, shame on me."

She laughs sharply. It's got an edge of self-mockery to it. "That's the one," she says. "It would have been more than I could bear if I'd taken him back and he turned around and cheated on me again. But then he tried to take his life."

I made a fool of myself making a judgment call on her and I don't want to stumble twice in one conversation, but I would've liked to say that doing something like that to yourself, just to make somebody else feel guilty, is one of the worst things a person can do and she certainly ain't got nothing to be sorry for. I also don't say it because I know there's more to come and I don't want to add to her distress.

"He did a lousy job of it," she says. "He ran a car into a tree. Totaled the car but didn't kill himself. Left him a cripple from the waist down. He's in a wheelchair."

She's staring at me, the awful thought trembling there

between us like she was shouting out loud, *Well, he isn't going to have much of a chance to fuck around on the side now, is he?*

The unspoken words drain the energy from both of us and we sit there like a couple of rag dolls for a long time until I finally break the spell by clearing my throat.

I'm still staring at her, listening to this story she's telling me, waiting for the punch line.

"That's right, I took him back."

"Even after what he done?"

"What he did was act like an aging ram chasing one last ewe through the clover."

"But—"

"I never said he stopped loving me or me him. If I'd been smarter when he first told me he'd fallen in love with another woman, I'd have told him to take a thousand bucks and a long weekend, or maybe spend the thousand bucks on a top professional lady in some hotel on the Loop where she might teach him the difference between love and lust."

"That sounds a little cynical."

"Which is because the society's more than a little hypocritical. The French are romantic. The Italians are hot-blooded. Even the English know how to be naughty and discreet. But American men have to throw over wife, home, family, lifestyle . . . the whole shebang . . . and marry someone else just because it's more honorable to tell a wife that you've fallen madly in love with another woman than that you want another piece of ass now and then."

The way she mixes genteel speech with gutter language, which somehow ain't even offensive coming from her mouth, has me rocking.

"Madly in love," she says. "Isn't that a crock of you know what?"

Apparently shit is the one word she don't like to say.

"Wouldn't anybody say, the way you're acting, taking

care of your crippled ex-husband the way you're doing, that you're madly in love?"

"I'm not madly in love, Mr. Flannery—"

"Jimmy," I says, butting in, figuring with all these intimate revelations she's giving me, it's about time she calls me by my first name the way practically everybody does.

"I'm sanely in love, Jimmy. I'm in love because of the good times, the old times. We're back together a year now and that's that. Harry's in therapy and doing pretty well, though the doctors don't hold out much hope that he'll ever walk again. I'll take care of the poor sorry sonofabitch until he dies or I die. One or the other."

She still ain't told me how she got into the life and I suppose she figures it's none of my business. She's laid out her story and where the pressures would've piled up. Expenses every time she turns around.

"I was already in the life part-time, Jimmy," she says, like she's reading my mind. "I got used to the money and you've got to remember, I never walked the streets or worked the bars. I saw no reason, with all the added expense, to give it up."

"How'd your husband take that?"

"Pride comes in a hundred flavors, Jimmy. Maybe Harry's ready to accept what I do so we can live a decent, even comfortable life, more easily than he could accept the necessity of asking for welfare and food stamps. As long as I don't rub it in his face. As long as I make up lies about promotions, raises, overtime and bonuses. Who'd expect him to believe it if whispers ever reached his ears? I'm a respectable, attractive, middle-aged, middle-class, college-educated whore. My husband knows but pretends not to know. My clients are all very nice men and Frank Delvin was one of my dearest."

Somebody comes out on the little porch at the back of the house and calls out, "Fay!"

I look up and it's Lou Cleary standing there. "There's somebody I'd like you to meet."

"You'll excuse me for asking," I says, "but do you work for Cleary?"

"He doesn't own a contract. He acts as a nonexclusive agent. I pay him a fee per client, just like an actress pays her representative," she says.

She gets up and kisses me on the corner of the mouth where there's a little smear of chicken grease.

"Mmm," she says, "spicy," and walks away with her hips shifting one way and the other, slow and easy. A sexy, compassionate, respectable lady of a suitable age to pleasure an older man.

11

"Ain't it funny," my old man says.

We're sitting around the dinner table, Mike and Charlotte, his wife, my mother-in-law, and Aunt Sada, who's back living with them temporarily because of some argument she had with her landlord, who proceeded to evict her from her apartment, and Mary and me and little Kathleen.

"Ain't it funny how here I am, lived most of my life in the Fourteenth, now living out in the suburbs, living in Mount Pleasant, and Jimmy, here, born and raised in the Fourteenth, lived most of his life in the Twenty-seventh, is going home to the Eleventh, ward of the mayors."

"I don't see what's so strange," I says. "Twenty years ago you advised me to move over to the Twenty-seventh because anybody with political ambitions wouldn't have a chance to run for alderman in the Fourteenth, George Lurgan being sure to pass it on to his son."

"I remember giving you that good advice," Mike says.

"But young George ain't the alderman," I says. "Hilda Moskowitz has got the job, stole it right out from under the nose of the Irish the same year Janet Canarias copped the seat in the Twenty-seventh. So look at it one way, I could've stayed back there in the Fourteenth, just like you stayed back in the Fourteenth, and still worked as a precinct captain for the party in the Twenty-seventh, just like Delvin was the warlord and alderman from the Twenty-seventh even though he lived in the Eleventh."

"He had an accommodation address in the Twenty-seventh and a long history of service to the party. Also I thought it best that you should get to know your neighbors and as many people as you could in the ward and there ain't no better way to do that than live in it. Where else and how else could you have got the attention of a Chinaman as powerful as Chips Delvin? Where else could you've got a job like the one you've got?"

I'm about to say I could've done without working down in the sewers for all them years, wading through the muck and mire, but Mary coughs into her hand and then Kathleen imitates her with a little cough and everybody laughs. Another quarrel between Mike and me has been averted.

"Anyway, it's an omen, you moving into Delvin's old house in Bridgeport," Mike says.

I don't have to ask him what he means, though this is the first time I ever knew that my old man might have ambitions for me concerning higher office, even the chair on the fifth floor of City Hall.

"What do you think of the house?" Aunt Sada asks.

"It's beautiful and it's old. Those nine-foot ceilings and cove molding. The hardwood floors are grand," I says.

"The heating system is going to need upgrading. The plumbing could do with a little work as well, I'm sure," Sada says.

"It needs painting and wallpapering," Charlotte chimes in.

There's a lot of work to be done, the women agree.

I'm thinking that there's going to be many, many weekends when I'm going to be working on that old house.

I guess Sada sees that I'm already in a little distress, talking about moving into Delvin's house with his bones hardly cold in the ground.

"What do you think about Leo Lundatos showing up at the funeral?" Aunt Sada asks, changing the subject but not changing it to anything else but politics. Which is okay with me. She's as much a political creature as my old man or me, maybe more, her late husband, Manny Spice, having been a major figure in the Socialist Party. Since Manny and the party was closed out in a two-party town, she ain't forgot and takes every opportunity to ridicule the administration, the parties, and to drag up old grudges.

"Well, why shouldn't he?" Mike asks. "Didn't he know Delvin? Hadn't they come up together as young men?"

"Lundatos is almost a generation younger than Delvin, you figure twenty years to be a generation," Sada says. "Lundatos is more like your age."

"I ain't as old as Leo the Lion," my old man protests.

"Well, he's like seventy, maybe seventy-one or -two, is all I'm saying. He was never on a local career track anyway."

"The old mayor had his eye on him."

"But Lundatos had his eyes on federal office right from the start.

"What are you trying to say here, Sada?" Mike asks.

"I'm saying that Lundatos didn't have any reason to go to the funeral of a man a generation older than him and he didn't have any reason to go because he was running for office. His running days are over after this last congressional defeat."

"You're hitting a very long ball here," Mike says. "What makes you think the Lion's hung up his guns?"

"The man's got . . . what . . . sixty-two counts of fraud, theft, abuse of power, malfeasance, and misfeasance in the indictment against him."

"Which they ain't totally thrashed out as yet," Mike says.

"There's sixty-two counts against him but most of them are minor matters, practically breaches of etiquette."

"There's an even thirty felony counts," Sada says.

"You know how the lawyers work," Mike comes right back. "They want to sue somebody for leaving a rake hidden tines-up in the grass along a public right-of-way? So they sue the homeowner what left it there, the store what sold the rake, the company what manufactured it, the city what failed to send an inspector out to every empty lot to check for such dangers, and so on and so on."

Aunt Sada raises a finger, indicating she's got something to say here, but Mike barrels right on.

"So what they done here was they got these catchall charges like how many times Lundatos used the mails or the telephone to execute this alleged scheme to defraud Congress and the United States by calling crystal lion paperweights—"

"At a hundred and sixty bucks a pop," Sada snaps.

"—mistaking ballpoint pens—"

"Fancy fountain pens . . . Mont Blancs . . . at a hundred and fifty bucks each."

"—as Bics at twenty dollars a gross for office use."

"Also you've got a couple of obstruction-of-justice charges," Sada says.

"Like what?"

"Like tampering with a witness, by which is meant that he asked this retired congressional employee not to tell investigators about some work he did for Lundatos around his D.C. apartment for which he was paid out of office petty cash and this other ex-employee who was paid to engrave the bases of the crystal lions with suitable sentiments."

"The man wanted to show his appreciation to friends and neighbors."

"Also he's accused of putting certain people on the staff payroll, some of whom never bothered coming to work, which brings up the corollary charge of conversion of public funds for the salaries of ghost employees. So, perhaps, there's one crime but two charges here, the way lawyers work, but that doesn't make the crime any less."

Charlotte and Mary have already lost interest in the conversation, and have gone off into the living room with Kathleen, to talk more about the new house. But I'm enjoying every bit of the match between my father and Aunt Sada, of which Aunt Sada is way ahead on points.

"Howsomever, you'll admit," Mike says, "that sorting out what could be considered felonies and all the charges resulting from the execution of those felonies, it boils down to they got maybe four legitimate charges against him.

"One. He used office money to buy about twenty crystal lions which he had engraved and give to friends and associates.

"Two. Over a period of seven years sixteen thousand dollars—"

"Sixty thousand," Sada says, correcting him.

"—was spent, unaccounted and unvouchered, out of the allowances given to his office for petty-cash expenditures.

"Three. Apparently he'd used campaign funds to pay the leases and garaging expenses on vehicles which might've been for him and his family's personal use.

"Fourth and last. He'd put two, possibly three friends and relatives—"

"Eleven. Count them. Eleven."

"I ain't going to dispute. Let's say he put a couple of old friends, maybe a niece or a cousin, on the payroll. Somebody's got to do the work, why shouldn't it be somebody he knows and feels comfortable with?"

"Sure, why not?" Sada says. "Especially if several of them never showed up for work and two, at least, might be dead."

"I'm not condoning him buying these crystal lions and charging them to the government," Mike says, "but, looking at it one way, it's easy to imagine this big, hulking, glowering hard-nosed old pol fondling a glass statue of a

lion in his huge paws and thinking how this one or that one
is going to be so pleased getting this token of his gratitude
and esteem from his congressman. Though a paperweight
might not seem like much, it shows that Lundatos has a
good heart."

It's one of Mike's finest fairy tales.

"I can even see him passing by his secretary's desk in the
outer office," Sada says, in a tone of voice that matches
Mike's voice of gentle understanding, "feeling in his
pocket for some cash and not finding much walking-around
money. So he dips into the cash box for a hundred, two
hundred, like a kid looking for lunch money but, you've got
to admit, the least he could've done was drop an IOU in the
tin just to keep things neat.

"So sixty thousand. You say it was sixty thousand?"

"That's right."

"So sixty thousand over . . . how many years since he's
been chairman?"

"Fifteen."

"Fifteen into sixty adds up to about four grand a year or
three hundred bucks a month—"

"Three hundred and thirty-three."

"For Christ's sake, Sada, can't you cut me a little slack
here. You got to be so exact?"

She smiles sweetly.

"Okay, I don't claim three hundred and thirty-three
bucks a month over fifteen years is peanuts but it's nothing
compared to the millions the savings and loans stole from
the taxpayers, at which time the bureaucrats turn around
and hire the same accountants, lawyers and administrators
what was in on the original frauds to head up the Recovery
Trust Commission which is selling off the foreclosed properties. Give me a break."

Sada looks at me. She's confused. How and when did
Mike switch the subject from the charges against Lundatos
to the S&L scandal? She ain't used to Mike's slippery
ways.

"There's a lot of talk about holding our politicians up to certain standards," Mike goes on in this oily voice, "and I'm as ready as the next guy to do that if somebody'll show me the benchmarks."

"Huh?" Sada says.

"I mean we got one guy in Congress what's got one of the best records in the House on women's affairs and he's up on charges of grabbing female assistants from behind and giving them hugs and kisses by the water cooler. Which sounds innocent enough until this teenager comes along and accuses him of giving her a lot more than hugs and kisses on the office desk."

"Couch," Sada says as though correcting his fancies has become automatic and compulsive.

"At which time you got to give it another look. Unless, of course, you figure a seventeen-year-old girl ain't a lot different in appeal, except maybe more so, than an eighteen-year-old woman."

Sada winces like she's taken a body blow and I think Mike's maybe got her down for the count, but she's only catching her breath. She comes back with, "On the matter of amorous advances. Leo the Lion's got two of those against him, too."

"Unfounded allegations," Mike says. "Anyway it's all over for him now. These are all matters you'd reasonably expect to go away now that he ain't been returned to office."

"Which is exactly what I said," Aunt Sada says, not knowing who won the bout. "I said there was no reason for Lundatos to be at Delvin's funeral. He had other things than paying respect in mind."

"What do you mean?" Mike asks. "Spit it out for God's sake."

Aunt Sada gives me a look.

"These things aren't going away. Lundatos is still engaged in damage control. If he'd won his seat back like he was so sure he would, he might've hoped he'd proved his strength dramatically enough to back off Republicans who are out to get his head. Even if he lost, like he did, he might've thought they'd forget all about him."

"But nobody's forgetting about nobody in this Congress," I chimes in.

"You've got that right, Jim," Aunt Sada says. "The jackasses are going after the elephants, so the elephants are going after the jackasses. So what we have is a man still scrambling to stay out of jail. He's looking for a power base. He's looking for allies."

"So?" Mike almost yells, he's getting so frustrated with her pussyfooting around

"He was there to size up our Jimmy here," Sada says.

I bust out laughing.

Charlotte, Mary and Kathleen come in from the living room to see what's so funny.

My father's nodding and Sada's smiling like she just crowned me king.

"What could I do for Lundatos in his troubles?" I asks.

"You've got your ways of finding things out, Jimmy, and everybody knows it. That might be a valuable skill that Lundatos might find useful."

"I don't think so, Aunt Sada," I says.

Just then the phone rings.

Sada grins as though she knows that it is a prediction coming true even as we speak.

I go to the phone and a woman's voice asks for me and when I say it's me on the line she hands it over to a man whose growl I can't mistake.

"Mr. Flannery," Lundatos said, "would it be possible for you to meet me over at Schaller's Pump for lunch tomorrow about noon?"

12

Schaller's Pump is one thing that don't change.

It's a tavern what's been the drinking and eating club for the Eleventh Ward Democratic Party there in Bridgeport for as long as me and my old man can remember. It's right across the street from the party headquarters, in which anybody is hardly ever there.

A new bunch of old-timers, what look like the last batch of old-timers, with thatches of white hair like thistledown, sit around in the beer-smelling gloom, cutting up touches with the waitresses and the bartenders, lying to one another about triumphs fifty years old and inventing dreams for the future of this candidate and that made up on the spur of the moment.

When I walk in with my old man, who wanted to come along and no reason why he shouldn't, Lundatos is sitting at the largest table surrounded by a dozen or more of these admirers, who don't give a rat's ass that a bunch of idiots in their champion's own bunch hung him out to dry.

Lundatos greets me, though he don't stand up to do it, and I invite him to shake hands with my father.

"You got a comer in your boy, here," Lundatos says,

which makes me feel like I'm a prizefighter looking to be a contender.

My father nods and takes a chair when one is offered, ordering a beer and a corned beef on rye with sauerkraut from the waitress, who snatches his order from the air on the fly.

"We've been talking about Washington and the Beltway," Lundatos says, after we been introduced around to the men at the table, most of whom Mike and me already know.

"Whatsamatter these people, they got no loyalty?" Dennis Bochos, who'd sell his mother for a nickel, says, making points with the designated leader of the afternoon even though there's no longer any reason for him to make points with anybody. Him being out of the loop and the Loop and Beltway and every other inner sanctum of information and power in the country.

"They got no understanding of tit for tat," says Cocky Jameson, a guy with a crooked grin and a blinking eye, who always seems to be around, though nobody knows how he got there. He's got a habit of tossing in a remark from time to time meant to do nothing else but stir the pot.

"They got no understanding of how a man's supposed to do business," pipes up Beanie Bennett, who was Delvin's driver for years . . . though there wasn't much driving to do the last few . . . who's there maybe angling for another driver's job though he shouldn't be trusted to drive anything faster than a horse and wagon.

"You was right to tell them to shove it, Leo," says Billy Murphy, who makes his living running errands for anybody and everybody, though he ain't so fast of foot any more, having passed the age of ninety a couple of years back.

"God bless you, son," says Lundatos. This from a man of seventy to a man over ninety.

"You done right to defy them."

"Make no deals."

"They'll never go ahead with the hearings."

Everybody pitches in his golden coin of support and loyalty, hoping for who the hell knows what.

There's several suits sitting at a smaller table nearby, there to advise Lundatos should he need advice and provide protection should he be attacked.

After more than a year of keeping a low profile, I wonder why Lundatos is suddenly making public appearances in places where he knows he's going to be noticed and mobbed with admirers. And I'm wondering why he feels it necessary to have what the Mafia would call his *consiglieri* around to field any questions he might not be able to answer.

Lundatos focuses on me and says, "You didn't order anything to eat, Jimmy."

"I didn't know when and if we was going to have our talk," I says.

"Oh, yes, right here and now, if that's agreeable to you. In fact I was waiting for you to arrive before I ordered for myself. I always like to break bread the first time I have a chance to get to know somebody."

He looks around the table until even the slowest of the old-timers get the message and scatter back to their own tables, where flat beer and chilling burgers are waiting for them.

The waitress comes back, but she ain't got my father's sandwich. She's shrewd enough to know she don't yet know where he's going to be seated. She's standing there like a skinny bird on a fence waiting for me and Lundatos to order.

"No reason why you shouldn't sit in on this, Mike," Lundatos says, very generous and all, "unless you'd rather sit with your old friends."

Mike reads it right. Lundatos ain't asking him to go and he's not asking him to stay. He's actually giving him the choice but he'd like it better if it was just him and me. Mike decides to stay anyhow.

"I'll have my sandwich here," Mike tells the waitress.

Lundatos orders a corned beef on rye with sauerkraut and a beer, a subtle homage to my father which he knows ain't lost on either one of us. I order a salad with bleu cheese dressing and, not being a drinking man, a ginger ale instead of a beer.

"Eating hearty, I see," Lundatos says, making a little joke there.

"My wife, Mary, gets on me about eating red meat and so on," I says, by way of explanation. "She used to be a nurse over to Passavant."

"I had my appendix taken out at Passavant when I was a boy," Lundatos says, by way of showing we got things in common.

It's what people do, finding every little connection they can, so it'll feel like two people just met have known each other half their lives.

So we go on like that, remembering this and that, things we both know something about, a hot dog stand here and a candy store there, right through lunch.

Every once in a while Lundatos, with a glance, invites my old man to jump into the conversation.

I'm on my second ginger ale and he's on his fourth beer since I got there, when Lundatos leans forward and says, "You can do me a favor, Jimmy."

"All you got to do is ask."

"I need a right-hand man."

"You'll excuse me for saying so, but why would a man like yourself have to go trolling for a right-hand man when you got so many friends?"

He looks old and sad-eyed all of a sudden.

"You leave town and live somewhere else for nearly fifty years? You leave the old neighborhood and come back only now and then? Well, then you got plenty of friends in a foreign land but you ain't got many friends back home. None you can really trust to do right by you. You'd be surprised."

I nod my head and give it a little tilt, indicating that I know just what he means and regret the way friendships wither up and die if they ain't constantly watered nowadays.

It used to be you didn't see anybody for years and you bumped into them on the street and it was like ten, twenty years hadn't passed and it was only yesterday that you last met. But nowadays you got the telephone and E-mail and all these ways to keep in touch. So if either one of you don't keep in touch it's like you didn't want to keep in touch and that sinks in somehow. It ain't really true but it feels like it's true.

"It takes every day, every day, seeing people on the street, talking to them on the stoops and porches," Lundatos says. "How's your Aunt Becky's sore back? How's your brother, Sal? Doing his time upstate okay? You going to be all right for heating oil this winter? Well, don't you know that better'n me?"

He's working me shamelessly, understanding what all politicians understand, you don't have to worry about how outrageous you get with the flattery, the old Irish honey cake, Jewish chicken fat, Greek olive oil. You don't have to worry about being subtle. Lay it on with a trowel and people just suck it up. Flattered all to hell even if it lights up the sky like neon because you're taking the time to flatter them.

"You got it right," I says, which I figure is an okay reply though not outstanding.

"I envy the party workers, the little guys in the trenches."

"It'd be nice to stay down there in the warm mud," I says, working his metaphor to its natural conclusion, but I quickly segue into some stroking of my own and say, "but when you got a talent like you got a talent, Mr. Congressman, you got to go where destiny takes you."

He sighs one of them sighs what comes up from the toes and manages a misty look in the eye. A tear would've been too much, too soon.

"I got promoted to the leadership of the ward not too long ago," I goes on, cementing the relationship between us. "I thought I could keep in close touch with all the people in my precinct."

"But you can't," he says, adding his thought to mine.

"That's right, you can't," I says.

"You think you can but you can't," Lundatos says.

"Amen to that," Mike says, not wanting to be left out.

We sit there quiet for a minute, chewing over the melancholy facts of life in the service of the people.

"So I need a friend, Jimmy," Lundatos says, finally breaking the silence.

"How about them friends of yours sitting over there?" I asks.

"One's a lawyer from Washington. If I left him here, he couldn't find his way back to the hotel. The one next to him's a Washington accountant. The one wearing the three-piece suit is my Chicago attorney. I don't think he could find his way out of here, either, without he called a cab. The next one is a Chicago accountant. I don't even know him. They talk to each other. They don't talk to me except to say good morning and good night."

"Don't I recognize the big man with the white hair?" Mike says.

"Fred's the closest thing I got to a friend. He's my driver in Washington, but he was born and raised in the Seventh, alongside the steel mills."

"Fred Hennesy. I thought I knew him," Mike says.

"Old Fred's a little past it," Lundatos says, letting us know how loyal he is to people what are loyal to him.

"Well, I can see, maybe, that you might need somebody," I says, "But I still don't see why you thought about me."

"Old Delvin was your Chinaman? Well, he was my Chinaman, too, except I didn't make my way through city politics. I went by way of county and state. But I always asked his advice, because he knew more about how the cogs and wheels worked than just about anybody around."

I nod because I can't say no to that.

"We've been in touch this last year, year and a half," Lundatos says. "You know when I came back from Washington I bought a house just down the block from your house?"

"My house?"

"What was Delvin's house. He give it to you, didn't he?"

I'm about to ask him how the hell he knows that because the settlement of the estate ain't yet been entered into the public record when he says, "Delvin told me his intentions."

He wants me to know just how intimate he'd been with Delvin and in what high regard Delvin obviously held him, telling him all his private business the way he did.

"So now we're neighbors," he says. "You're going to move into that grand old house, ain't you?"

"It looks that way. My wife is already thinking about new wallpaper."

"It's going to be a costly venture, remodeling that old house," he says.

Oh, oh, I think. I hope he ain't going where I think he's going with this. I hope he ain't going to offer me the cash equivalent of a crystal lion or a Mont Blanc pen.

"Maybe your destiny's calling you," he goes on.

"How's that, you don't mind my asking?" I says.

"There's no reason for you to stay on as committeeman of the Twenty-seventh Ward."

"You don't have to live in the ward to be its leader," I says.

"Well, I know that, Jimmy. I just meant that there's better launching pads for someone like yourself than the Twenty-seventh. I'm also thinking that you're the kind of politician likes to talk to his constituents each and every day, meeting them in taverns like this, passing the time of day on the street corners, and I'm thinking you could become the committeeman in this ward, in the Eleventh, the ward of the mayors, no trouble at all."

"Johnny O'Meara's the warlord and alderman here."

"He's not well and wants to put work and troubles aside."

"I got the Twenty-seventh, with Delvin's blessing. Why would I want to take the chance, even if O'Meara gives me his, that some ambitious local don't challenge me anyway?" I asks.

"I'm telling you that you wouldn't be taking a chance," he says, and then he drops the reason for the meeting. "Especially not with me the alderman from the Eleventh."

I'm feeling like a fighter what's been hit a couple of hard shots to the head. I'm muddled and I need some room.

"Begging your pardon, Congressman, but you're a Greek. How do you expect to win an Irish ward?" I says. It's the first thing that comes to my mind.

"Are you forgetting my wife of almost forty years is Irish? You forgetting I got four kids who're half Irish and I don't know how many grandchildren who got Irish blood along with Greek blood in their veins? You forgetting Johnny O'Meara's my cousin through marriage? I'm not worried about can I win. You worried can I can?"

"You've still got some problems facing you if they decide to go ahead with them indictments against you."

"We're negotiating them away even as we speak," he says. "Delay is a weapon and time is on my side. The longer they screw with White House corruption and FBI incompetence, the better off I am. The longer the Republicans stonewall some Democrat from going after some Republican for sexual harassment, for hugging and kissing little girls, the harder it's going to be for them to sell a tale of moral outrage against me for putting my cousin on the payroll or taking some cab money out of the office petty cash."

I fan my hands out to the sides, saying I don't want to get into a debate.

He leans toward me, the lion fixing the lamb with his killer's eye.

"I got to do this, Flannery. I got to show the flag the only

way I can. I got to show them I ain't done. They still got to
reckon with me even if I only got a Chicago ward for a
base to start with. What I'm offering you is a chance to join
a winning team. Lundatos and Flannery. Me the alderman
and you the committeeman. And next time around, you the
alderman, if you want it."

And you the mayor I'm thinking. But he don't say that
and neither do I.

"You the alderman of the Eleventh, the mayors' ward,"
he says, spinning dreams. "Think about it. I got to go."

He's up in a flash, shaking my hand, shaking Mike's
hand, peeling off two twenties from a potato roll to pay for
the lunch, sticking a finger in the air to call his mob and out
the door.

13

"What the hell was that?" Mike says.

He's as stunned as me.

I look around. The old-timers has thinned out, only a couple left playing pinochle at the corner table at the back. A couple of younger workingmen, out of work, are bellied up to the bar. It's the quiet part of the afternoon between lunch and early supper. The light's the thin light of afternoon when taverns look like churches and I just been offered what could be the best political deal of my life. And just as well might not.

"I think you just got made an offer," he adds.

"But what kind of offer was it?" I says. "What's an ex-congressman doing reaching down into the stew of ward politicians looking for a running mate?"

"But that's just it, don't you see, Jimmy? You ain't considered just another one of the regular ward heelers. You're known as an independent, your own man, beholden to no one. Especially now, with your old Chinaman dead and gone, you don't owe no favors to nobody. You're an asset to anybody what wants to run for office on the platform that he's an outsider without ties or favors owed."

"That's a lot of damn foolishness," I says. "I don't care who you are, if you're running for office, you got obligations to somebody unless you was hid away in a cave for the last twenty years."

My father's grinning.

"That's just what old Leo the Lion intends to claim. He's been away in the caves of D.C., inside the Beltway, lost to his own people. Now the son of Chicago's home to see what needs doing and ready to start doing it."

"You think he hopes he can build a new power base fast enough to head off these hearings after all?"

"No matter what he might've done or what he's been accused of doing back in D.C., Lundatos was one of the most powerful men in the country not long ago and he can still chew up rabbits for a snack and pick his teeth with the bones of wolves," Mike says. "There's some people might think that whatever happened in D.C. don't matter one helluva lot here in Chicago. All the voters know is that one of their own, doing business the way business has been done for a couple of hundred years, might have his feet put to the fire by a bunch of assholes who don't understand Chicago manners and customs."

"But he got beat for reelection last time out," I says.

"Because the district includes the suburbs and other venues besides central Chicago. We're talking hometown, here. He runs, he wins."

"He's past seventy. That's too old to start all over again."

My old man points a finger at me. "Is that so? Let me tell you, sonny, the minute Lundatos takes his seat as alderman from the Eleventh, the mayor knows he's got a rival as tough as Fast Eddie Vrdolyak was to Mayor Washington, a power to be reckoned with, a man what could pick the city of Chicago off the tree like it was a peach. He'll be the lion that roars. And the politicians throughout the state and country, knowing damn well that Chicago and Illinois is still big players in the presidential sweepstakes, are going to think twice before they yank the lion's tail."

He's ready to celebrate right then and there, but he sees the expression on my face and asks, "So what about it, Jim? You going to grab the offer?"

It hits me hard right then and there how much I depended on Delvin to give me the word. Even when we was at sixes and sevens, I always knew I could go to him and get the best counsel. That he always had my best interests at heart, even if I didn't always take his advice.

Mary's the first person I talk with, if I got to talk something through, but there's subtleties here that could be hard to explain to her because her idea of what's right and wrong is a little more unforgiving than mine.

Of course, my first and best adviser had always been the man sitting right across the table from me but I'm afraid his ambitions for me is clouding his vision this time.

"I think I got to do a little more homework before I make up my mind," I says.

14

First thing Monday morning I go down to the new Harold Washington Library, which is a beauty.

Ordinarily I ain't got as much time for reading as I'd like but at least I got a library card and I stop in for a browse every chance I get, having got into the habit when I started taking night classes in English and political science. Which is not to say I never read a book in my life before that.

I get out the *Weekly Congressional Record* going back to when Lundatos started having his difficulties with the Ethics Committee.

I also read commentaries in the *Chicago Tribune* and the *Chicago Sun-Times*. Also the *New York Times,* the *Christian Science Monitor* and the *Wall Street Journal*.

Of all the wrong things a politician can do, there's two stand out, that're up there on the top of the list and they're not exactly what you'd think.

Like it ain't picking the public pocket that gets everybody up in arms, it's *lying* about it after you get caught. It's not playing around with women you shouldn't be playing around with, it's *covering up* after some woman or women blow the whistle on you.

In these situations, nowadays, a person's more likely to be forgiven for dipping into the till than for tickling the women.

I ain't going to take a position here, except to say that rape, indecent assault and even persistent sexual harassment should be prosecuted to the limit, but asking somebody out for a date more than once, more than twice, or kissing a lady . . . no tongues, no tongues! . . . could be rude and clumsy but ain't a prison offense. I can't help but think that a lot of these ladies bringing charges are just grabbing a ride on this new gravy train.

Anyways, I read the arguments pro and con, which pretty much break down along party lines. No big surprise.

The trouble is I ain't any farther along making up my mind when I finish reading all this stuff than when I started. Also no big surprise.

What is a big surprise is when a deep, soft voice says, "How's it hanging, Jimmy?" which is a man's greeting, but when I turn around Mabel Halstead's standing there, leaning over and smiling at me.

For a minute I don't know how to handle the situation. Am I supposed to reply in kind, like Mabel was still Milton, the cop I used to know before he had his sex-change operation? Or am I to be more careful and answer her like I would if she was a lady friend?

She's dressed in jeans, a wide red belt with a silver buckle and a white blouse opened low enough so there's no doubt is she a woman if you took a good look. Yet it's hard to know are you meeting a man what is effeminate, maybe homosexual, or a woman what is a lipstick lesbian, or what.

"You look confused, Jimmy."

"No, no, Mabel. You just caught me by surprise."

"Last time we met I was in a pants suits and the time before that in a dress," she says.

"And the time before that you was in a dress when you knocked Vellitri's muscle on their ass."

"And weren't those two surprised," she laughs. "You wanted to talk to me, Jimmy?"

"I wanted to thank you for coming to pay your respects to Delvin, but you got away before I could get to you."

"He was a friend," she says.

"I looked for you at the funeral feast."

"I didn't go. I didn't want to draw attention. Can I buy you a coffee? There's a nice coffeehouse around the corner."

Mabel's sitting there with a cappuccino and I'm sitting there with something called a Rocket, which is a double espresso with chocolate and whipped cream. Also she's brought back a plate of little pastries.

"Mary sees what I'm eating here, she wouldn't be very happy," I says.

"Half the fun of sinning is putting it over on your nearest and dearest," Mabel says.

"How did you get friendly with Delvin?" I asks.

"He summoned me for a consultation."

"In your capacity as Janet Canarias's aide?"

"I don't work for Janet any more and you know it. Delvin had been asked to talk with me about my new enterprise. Isn't that what you want to talk to me about?"

"It's been suggested that I might mediate any conflict of interest which might have come up concerning that."

She cocks her head at me in this winsome way, which is a good trick for a woman over six feet.

"What?"

"Every once in a while I notice your grammar smooths out and you deliver a sentence or a phrase that might have come out of the mouth of a lawyer," she says.

"I ain't trying to be somebody I'm not," I says.

"I'm not suggesting," she says. "I'm just saying that you

might not know that you're becoming somebody you haven't been up to now."

"Christ, Halstead, you can talk plainer than that," I says.

"Is it getting to you? The influence? The power?"

"Maybe it's just that night school is starting to take," I says.

"I heard about the offer from Lundatos," she says.

"For God's sake, you know about that already?"

"Beers got ears," Mabel says, meaning . . . well, I don't got to explain that, do I? Have conversations in taverns and saloons and you can just bet you broadcasted the news over the eary network.

"You told Janet yet?" I asks.

"Oh, she already knew when I called her up to tell her."

"Can we talk about your situation?" I asks.

"My situation is simple. This is a free enterprise system. Everybody's entitled to go into business for his or herself. That's what I've done."

"But you're stepping on toes."

"I don't think the Justice Department is going to come in here looking at Cleary's call service monopoly."

"He don't run all the ladies in the territory he's staked out, does he?"

"Of course not. He doesn't bother with bar girls or streetwalkers. He had a very choice and select stable of companions."

"Which he claims he's been very good to over the years and expects a return from on his investment."

"Which is what?"

"Compassion and risk."

"Does he claim that I'm stealing the women away with unfair practices?"

"Well?" I says, letting him have the ball.

"All I'm doing, Jimmy, is trying to rescue them from their own lack of organization and business acumen. Most of these aren't wayward women driven into the life by drugs or coercion. But that doesn't mean they have any more understanding of finances or the ways in which they can insure their old age than the average housewife. Which isn't much."

"So just what is it you're doing for them?" I asks.

"I'm offering a package of financial services, including money management, health insurance, annuities and personal security."

"That last one there, personal security? Some people could say you're running a protection racket."

"Similar to the protection rackets pimps run on their whores?" she says. "Reverse security. Promising protection from themselves? No, no, Jim, that's not what I'm doing. I don't threaten these women with physical violence. I make them an offer based upon sound fiscal policy."

"Just how do you work that?"

"I run a check on them. Their lifestyle. Being a cop comes in handy. I know how to go about it. They need psychological counseling, they have a drug problem, anything like that, I can see they get it. I assess their earning capacity and project an earning curve. I tailor-make a program of savings and investment."

"What's your cut?"

"Less than Cleary's. Less than any pimp on the streets. But that's not even the most persuasive improvement I offer."

"What's that?"

"I give them a chance to participate in the decisions that will affect everything they do. I empower them, Jimmy, and that's the best thing a person can do for another person. We'd all be charity cases if the Clearys of the world had their way."

I sit there in the café. My Rocket's gone cold.

"Do you want another one of those?" Mabel asks.

"No, thanks. That was plenty," I says.

"So now you know what I'm doing," she says. "Delvin flexed his muscle on Cleary's behalf but it wasn't much. He did it only because he was getting favors from Cleary or, rather, women from Cleary's stable. Are you flexing your muscle for similar reasons?"

"I don't know how to answer that," I says.

Mabel can read my face. "I'm sorry I asked," she says.

"All of a sudden the issues that get handed to me ain't about trimming a tree limb what's blocking some old lady's sun in the morning or making sure some abandoned woman with kids has got heat in the winter. All of a sudden Janet's telling me she's got militant citizens demanding that she clear the hookers off the strolls and ex-cops are asking me to mediate disputes over call girl territory."

"The next step up the ladder and you'll be asked to decide between little business and big business, big tax relief and big welfare. You remember what Dorothy said in *The Wizard of Oz*?"

"What's that?" I notice I'm saying what's that a lot in this conversation.

"Toto, I don't think we're in Kansas any more."

15

So nothing's really settled about none of these things which has been shoveled on my plate.

The move from the apartment to the house.

The offer to be Lundato's running mate in the Eleventh.

The business differences between Cleary and Halstead, these two ex-cops what has become pimps, no matter how you want to look at it. Which is not to say there ain't pimps and pimps, just like there's prostitutes and prostitutes, what come in all sizes, colors and persuasions. Not all of them necessarily bad.

Mike comes over for a conference Friday night. Charlotte begs off because she's really not much for politics, but Sada's there because she's a political animal and you couldn't keep her away with horses.

Also I invite Janet Canarias to give me her input.

The offer from Lundatos is first on the agenda.

"I wouldn't like it, you leaving the Twenty-seventh," Janet says. "I wouldn't like not stopping in to talk when you're using my storefront. I wouldn't like it not seeing you in the neighborhood. And I wouldn't like it you not being the committeeman in my ward any longer."

"Well, you could get one of your own people in the job," Mike says.

"My own people," Janet says, repeating what he said with an edge on it.

"Yes, your own people. I mean like the same way I'd say it to an Irishman, or an Italian or a Jew," Mike says. "People with the same persuasion you espouse, be it racial, political, generical or otherwise."

"Espouse?" I says. I don't question the generical because I ain't sure is it, isn't it, a real word.

He looks down his nose at me, like he's got a word or two in his vocabulary just as good as any of the new words I been throwing around since I started taking night classes in English.

"Sorry, Mike," Janet says. "I'm on the edge. Some church groups and some far-right conservative groups have joined the women in the neighborhood organizations to put pressure on me to move an ordinance forbidding the use of the sidewalks for illicit and immoral purposes."

"Don't they know if the police push here the bump'll come out there? Like a balloon filled with water? The action'll just go to another neighborhood. It won't make the hookers disappear," I says.

"They don't care about that. All they care about is moving it out of their neighborhoods."

"We ought to have it like it was back in New Orleans in Storyville," Sada says.

"Legalize prostitution?" Mary says, with some distress.

"Create a red-light district?" Janet adds.

"I never said that, though sex, like drugs, might be controlled better if it was decriminalized. Also, Storyville wasn't a district formed by direct law. The ordinance Commissioner Storey wrote said where houses of prostitution *couldn't* be."

"And created Storyville by default," Janet says.

"We play those games all the time," Sada says. "Interpreting the Constitution, we even look at things not specifically included and try to argue the case that anything not specifically *excluded* can be a constitutionally conferred liberty or right."

I'm afraid we're going to get into one of them long philosophical lectures what Sada loves to give, her being an unreconstructed socialist and all.

"I don't see how this is getting us any closer to Jimmy, should he, shouldn't he, take Lundatos up on his offer and run with him for committeeman of the Eleventh," Mike says.

"Which is now going to be his home," Janet says, "I can understand wanting to do that," she says, which shows how fair she can be, arguing against her own preference.

"The man's a crook," Sada says, getting back on the track with a bang.

"How can you say that?" Mike asks. "You're always touting justice. Well, this is still a nation of laws and this is still a country where a man's innocent until proven guilty."

"Okay, I take it back," Sada says. "He's *alleged* to be a crook with enough evidence to sink a ship. Even the voters from his own district couldn't swallow his protests and excuses and wouldn't vote him back into office. When Chicago voters—who have been known to reelect incumbents whose transgressions smelled to high heaven—fail to return a man to office, you can just imagine what a stink they think Lundatos made."

"Well, then, what do you think I should do?" I says.

"Tell him no," Sada says.

"You don't got to make a decision today," Mike says. "Give it a couple of days."

"Make it a week," Janet says.

"Make it ten days," Mary says. "We'll be moved into Bridgeport by then."

Which is the first I heard about *that*.

"Next?" Janet says.

"What next?" I says.

"The matter of the hookers on the strolls. Which also involves your attempts to adjudicate the dispute between Lou Cleary and Mabel Halstead."

"What dispute is this?" Mike asks.

I'd just as soon not, but Janet's already let the cat out of the bag, so I give them what they don't know about it a quick rundown of the situation.

Mary, having seen plenty in her job as a nurse and a volunteer down at the Family Planning Center, is what I'd call a compassionate pragmatist. Which is to say she's even less judgmental than I try to be, accepting people for what they are.

Sada's conflicted, being a socialist on the one hand who believes that the capitalistic, authoritarian society is what puts the pressure on unfortunate women to become prostitutes, one way or another, and is much against it. And on the other hand is a militant feminist who believes that women should be allowed to make their own decisions about how they use their bodies and the price they charge for that use, marriage being at one end of the scale and fifty bucks a trick at the other.

Janet is against prostitution because she knows the circumstances and conditions that usually force young girls and women into the life. At the same time she's libertarian and understands the danger of the government sticking its nose in the private business of people.

The only one who ain't got an opinion is my old man.

"It wouldn't be good to ask the police to have a sweep. It wouldn't be good to make a splash about it in the council chambers," Mike says, but don't say what would be good.

"So what can I do?" Janet asks. "I've tried to talk them into moving their action somewhere else or giving up the action altogether."

"I'll bet that got you a few laughs," I says.

"You're not going to get them to change their lives, you know," Mary says. "I've talked to hundreds of these girls and women, most of them still children, worn out by the time they're twenty, and what they'll tell you is that they like the life. And who am I to say that life on the streets might not be better than the life they had at home? I talk to social workers and they tell me, if you can't turn these kids around within six weeks after they hit the streets, you've lost them forever."

"They like the hardships? They like the danger?" Janet asks nobody in particular.

"It's like an adrenaline high," Mary says. "They get addicted to it as much as they get addicted to the drugs they start using."

"It's a problem too big for an alderman and ward leader," Sada says. "It's the bones of the society that need mending."

"But the problem I got is between two people who consider themselves entrepreneurs, doing good things for employees and clients alike," I says. "What Janet's got is a different problem, clearing the streets in the neighborhoods."

"Two different situations here," Mike agrees, nodding his head like the wise old man he sometimes is and sometimes ain't. "I got to think about your problem a little more, Jimmy," he goes on, "but about Janet's problem . . ."

We wait as he gets ready to enjoy his moment.

"You get the Catholic sisters from the nearest church or convent to go out there every evening, every night, taking up a collection for wayward girls and dropping a word here and there. Maybe they could even manage a conversion or the salvation of a soul or two but, primarily, their presence should convince the hookers to go someplace more suitable to do their business. Just by the nuns being there. It should maybe take a week."

16

There's one thing can bring speculation about should you do this or should you do that to a quick halt. Death.

I'm not saying the end of a life ends the consequences of the life but it sure twists your head around a hundred eighty degrees.

I get a call in the morning while I'm standing in the kitchen wondering what I should make for my breakfast, Mary not being at home, having dropped off Kathleen at the nursery school on her way over to Delvin's house.

I don't recognize the caller and he don't say. It's a man's voice, filtered through a handkerchief, I shouldn't be able to identify it the next time I hear it.

"You want to help yourself make up your mind?" he says.

"About what?"

"About the offer Lundatos handed you over to Schaller's Pump."

"How do you know about this offer?" I asks.

He laughs. It's harder to disguise a laugh than a speaking voice, but still I can't place him.

"Who is this?" I asks.

"Let's just say a friend," he says.

"So how can I help myself?" I asks.

"Take a drive over to the Eleventh. To Bridgeport."

"Yeah, to Bridgeport?"

He gives me an address on Lowe which is three blocks away from where Mary and me and Kathleen and Alfie's going to be living and which is where the old mayor used to live in the house he built for him and his wife when he first became city clerk.

"Fay Wray will be waiting for you," he adds.

"Any special time?" I asks.

"Suit yourself," he says, and hangs up.

Mary's already over in Bridgeport with Aunt Sada, Charlotte and Gloria Chapman, the female half of a salt and pepper couple, her husband, Calvin, having been the doctor in the clinic where Mary was volunteering her time when we first met after a bombing.

Mary's told me she don't want me over there helping out just yet. First she wants to sort out what furniture, lamps, drapes, paintings and so forth she wants to keep, which she'll offer to charities and which to friends . . . after I get to okay what she's decided, of course.

The truth is, at least the truth as I see it most of the time, is that men are a lot less interested in the inside of houses than women are. You could say that once upon a time this cavewoman thought it might be a good idea to hang some skins on the walls of the cave to keep the heat in and the man might have done the hanging but I don't think he cared if the hides matched or not.

You think of just about every couple you know. Who decides on the way the house is going to look? The wallpaper, the color of the paint, the pattern of the slipcovers. Five'll get you ten the women has the final say.

So, anyway, I got the car because Mary went over to Bridgeport in Gloria's station wagon.

I drive right over to Bridgeport, wondering what kind of mess I could be walking into.

The building the anonymous caller directs me to is one of them remodels where somebody took two three-flats right next door to one another, joined them at the hip with a new section, broke through the walls and made a handsome big flat out of the flats on either side of these mostly glass breezeways. There's bay windows in every room facing the street.

The frosted glass entrance door, with a fancy design of ladies in their nightgowns dancing around a pole and holding onto ribbons etched into it, is at the top of a short flight of three stone steps.

There's a very low-key brass plaque announcing that the first floor is occupied by the firm of Higgens, Huggins and Burke; and Parnell and Jones, a management corporation. The second floor is occupied by Davidian and Associates, Twenty-first Century Properties and Carteret Enterprises. It don't say what's on the third.

I walk up and try the door to the outer vestibule but it's locked. I'm about to take a step back to look up, checking to see if there's anybody up there looking down at me, when the door opener buzzes and I got to move fast to get it open in case they only give me the one buzz to release the catch.

The vestibule's got a marble floor and polished brass mailboxes built into one wall. There's no identification of whoever has the third floor here, either.

The inner door, also etched and frosted with more women in their nightgowns, is also locked.

I press the bell for the third floor and wait, knowing damn well it's going to get buzzed open. But first I hear one of them wheezing whistles the old speaking tubes make and I know that this feature of the building has refurbished and not replaced with intercoms.

"Yeah," I says, loud enough for anybody to hear.

Very faintly I hear a voice say, "Flannery?"

"Yes," I says, still talking pretty loud.

"Come on up. You'll have to walk."

The inner door clicks open.

There's a small elevator what's been added to the building, running up the central addition, but it's for tenant use only; you need a key. I guess you go visiting anybody on the third floor, and you got something heavy with you, they got to come down and get you. Whoever answered the speaker ain't going to give me that courtesy.

I climb the six flights of stairs up to the top floor, which ain't all that hard for me because I live on the third floor of the six-flat which I live in on Polk Street, but which I ain't going to be living in much longer.

There's a very fancy carved door at the top facing the elevator with a Judas hole surrounded by some brass filigree in the center of it and a big brass Victorian door knocker just below it.

I didn't really expect to find whoever buzzed me in waiting for me. I get an expectation, an intuition, whatever you want to call it, when I turn around to face the flight of stairs leading up to the roof. For a second there I'm about to go to the top and see what's there. Maybe I should've done exactly that but I don't. Instead, I turn back to the door and use the knocker.

I hear the faint snap of a latch at the top of the stairs. This time I don't hesitate. I make it to the top pretty quick. I put my shoulder against the door and push it open slow and easy. I step out onto the wooden catwalk, not knowing who could be waiting for me.

But nobody's waiting for me. There's a kind of cupola for decoration at each corner of the roof. I run to each one of them and look around them, figuring somebody could be hiding behind one of them, standing on the edge of the roof. Nothing. Then I run over to the fire escape, which I should've done in the first place, but there's nobody in sight.

So I go back downstairs and try the thumb latch. The

door's not locked. I walk into this room made entirely of glass on the side facing away from the street.

I take a closer look at the entrance. There's green plants in fancy pots all along one wall and a green wrought-iron and glass-topped breakfast set overlooking a garden down below with some glossy pamphlets on it. There's an open glass door at one end and a half-opened, hand-carved wooden door at the other.

I pick the side with the open glass door first.

The first room is like a sitting room or whatever you want to call it. Two overstuffed chairs, a couch, a coffee table and some floor lamps and side tables with more lamps on them. The pictures on the wall are what I'd call exotic but not exuberant, if you know what I mean.

The pictures in the first bedroom to the left are exotic and very exuberant and the murals in the adjoining bathroom, which is all marble and gold fixtures, even more so.

Going the other way there's a very large kitchen, all brass, chrome and glass, with granite counters.

The whole thing looks like what they used to call back in the twenties or thirties a love next.

There's nobody there. I call out three or four times, getting louder each time, but there's nobody there. It's really no surprise.

I don't get the feeling that anybody's actually living in the place day by day. It feels a lot like an office or a doctor's reception room, even the kitchen, which has only got enough appliances and utensils to make a cup of coffee or maybe heat up a frozen dinner.

Except for the plants in pots out in the glass room, there's no living plants around, just a lot of very expensive silk flowers, different kinds, arranged in vases, no two the same.

I go back through the atrium and through the wooden door to the other side of the apartment which is in the other building.

This place is a lot different. It's got a paneled living

room with burgundy leather furniture, glass-fronted book-cases on two walls, a dining room with a crystal chandelier over the table and a small room like what I see butlers use to serve from in the movies.

There's another small bedroom decorated in Scottish tartan. The bed is rumpled. There's a man's robe tossed on it and a pair of men's slippers, velvet with embroidered stag's heads on the toes, beside it.

There's not a sound in the whole flat.

Whoever spoke to me from up here when I was in the foyer ain't anywhere around. But I got the eerie feeling that I ain't alone.

There's a crumpled negligee on the floor in front of the door to the bathroom.

I go into the bathroom. She's in the tub. In about six inches of water. There's no blood that I can see but she's dead.

I check to see the floor's dry and kneel down to check her pulse with a finger at her throat. She's gone all right.

I dip my fingers in the water. It's still warm, so she ain't been laying there for too long but I don't know exactly how long.

Her eyes is just a little bit open like she's peeping at me through her eyelashes, having fun with me, flirting with me. Fay Wray, the middle-class housewife who supported herself and her once-faithful now-crippled husband by laying her no longer young body down for the use and comfort of lonely and otherwise unhappy aging men.

17

According to the book, I should've called the police and let them send the uniforms, who would then call the detectives.

I should've let them decide who was going to take jurisdiction.

But I don't. Instead I call the Downtown Precinct, Homicide Division, because Dominick Pescaro, an old friend of mine, who used to be the captain in my ward, has done good for hisself and is now an assistant chief, Homicide Central.

His assistant, a very nice lady by the name of Shirley Gionfrido, tells me he'll get back to me.

"This is very urgent," I says.

"What sort of urgency?" she asks.

"Somebody's been murdered."

"Well, that's not exactly an urgency around here, Mr. Flannery." When she calls me Mr. Flannery, it means she's in her official mode, ready to refuse all favors. "It's what we do, dealing with murder."

"This is a murder with special circumstances," I says.

"Where did this murder take place?"

"In Bridgeport."

"First you call the district station and they'll take it from there," she says.

"I know the drill, Shirley. What I need here is a little pre-investigation consultation."

"Am I to assume that there are politically sensitive circumstances surrounding this homicide?" she asks.

"You've hit the nail on the head," I says.

"Hold on."

In a minute Pescaro's on the line.

"I hope I ain't interrupting anything important," I says.

"I'm having breakfast at my desk," he says. "You're lucky I'm here at all."

"I took a chance and hit the jackpot," I says.

"So what's so urgent?"

"I got a call to come over to Bridgeport."

"What for?"

"To speak to someone who could help me make up my mind about an offer somebody gives me."

"Who was the someone?"

"I don't know for sure. A woman who sells her favors to aging gentlemen."

"She got a name?"

"She goes by the name Fay Wray."

"Like the actress what was in the original *King Kong*?" he asks.

"That's what she calls herself."

"So what did she tell you?"

"Nothing. She was in the bathtub. Dead."

"Shirley told me you said murdered. How do you know she was murdered?"

"It's the first thing that come to mind under the circumstances. Come look for yourself," I says.

"Why should I come look for yourself, a dead call girl in a bathtub? Go through the drill. The division cop'll call me if they need me."

"Congressman Leo Lundatos was the one made me the

offer. The suggestion give me by this anonymous caller
was that Fay Wray maybe had something to do with him."

"Oh-oh," Pescaro says. He hangs up.

I pick up the folders on the breakfast table and look them
over. They're health insurance plans and offerings for single-premium annuities. I put them in my pocket and sit
there wondering who it was dropped me in this pot of soup.

Did the somebody who called me kill Fay Wray or did
he just find her body after she was dead?

Did this somebody know something about Fay Wray and
Lundatos or was he paying off an old grudge, siccing the
dogs on a man who was already under attack? Was I the
dog this person picks because I got a reputation for uncov-
ering official cover-ups?

Or was it a panic call from somebody who wanted my
help and in the time it takes me to get over to Bridgeport,
the panic gets so bad it threatens to drown him and he takes
a powder.

I hear Delvin's voice like it's right in my ear.

"Don't waste your time supposing when you ain't got all
the facts," he says. "That's like a blind man feeling an elephant's leg and calling it a tree."

So I try not to think about it, but that ain't easy. Finally I
hear the tramp of feet coming up the last two flights of
stairs and three or four voices grumbling and complaining
about the climb.

I left the door open so they could walk right in and they
walk right in.

"Flannery! Show yourself!"

It's Francis O'Shea, the mean cop of the Mutt and Jeff
pair with Murray Rourke, the one you really got to watch,
playing the sweetheart.

I don't bother answering back. I just wait until they find
me.

"There you are," Pescaro says.

I don't even get up out of the chair.

"In the bathroom back there," I says.

Rourke and O'Shea go on through the living room into the bedroom and then into the bathroom as Pescaro sits down on the couch.

"In the tub!" I yells.

"How are you, Jimmy? Long time no see," Pescaro says.

"Well, you left the old precinct," I says.

"You weren't around much, either," he says, "and now I hear you're going to be moving into this neighborhood."

"But nothing as grand as this."

He looks around the room.

"Very tasteful," he says.

O'Shea comes back into the room.

"Why'd you yell she was in the tub? We could see she was in the tub," he says.

"Just trying to be helpful."

"Oh, yeah. You want to have a look, Chief?"

Pescaro gets to his feet.

"I might as well. You coming?" he says to me.

"I might as well, although I seen her once," I says.

"I'm surprised you wasn't in there feeling her up when we arrived," O'Shea says, like a nasty kid who'll say mean things just for the sake of saying mean things.

"You're going to have to learn to put a lid on that kind of remark," Pescaro says.

O'Shea looks hurt. "Hell, it's only Flannery."

I follow Pescaro to the bathroom door and O'Shea follows me.

"You find her like that?" O'Shea asks.

"I did."

"You didn't touch her?"

"No, I didn't."

"How do you know she was murdered like you said on the phone?" he asks. "How do you know she didn't slip and kill herself while she was taking a bath?"

"Then sits herself up?" Rourke says, taking the mickey out of his partner the way he sometimes likes to do.

"She don't look like a whore," O'Shea says, which I think is a surprising thing for him to say. He's seen it all and he's always acted like, from his point of view, anybody who gets involved in violent crimes, perpetrator or victim, is scum, deserving of no pity or respect.

"What does a whore look like?" I says. "She was a nice woman."

"Huh!" he grunts, his tender moment over.

"She was working to support a crippled husband."

"And six kids, three of them retarded, and an old mother, ninety-two, what's got liver cancer and Alzheimer's," he says, back to his old self altogether.

"You know her?" Pescaro asks, giving me a look like he expects me to deny ever having met her.

"Yes, I do, which is to say I met her once."

"She told you a lot about herself in one meeting."

"People do that."

"I know that, Flannery. It's one of your gifts."

I don't know if he's being sarcastic or what.

"When did this meeting take place?" he asks.

"At Delvin's funeral feast."

"Oh," he says, and frowns.

He turns away and walks back into the bedroom and I follow him. He stops and looks around. O'Shea comes with us, but Rourke stays behind.

O'Shea puts on a pair of latex gloves and starts poking around in the closet and the big chest of drawers.

"That the first time you met her?" Pescaro asks.

"First and last."

"Who introduced you?"

"We introduced ourselves over the potato salad."

"You trying to pick her up or her trying to pick you up?"

"Nothing like that. She wanted to talk to me about something."

"Am I going to have to put my foot on your chest and pry it out of your mouth with pliers?" he asks.

I can hear Rourke's voice, with that slightly hollow

sound hard surfaces make, coming from the bathroom, talking on a phone.

"I'm trying to cooperate here," I says.

"So tell me what you got to tell me without me holding your hand," Pescaro says. "Just tell me from the beginning. I'll jump aboard if I miss something."

"It all starts when I call up Diversey Funeral Home because Chips Delvin once mentioned to his housekeeper, Mrs. Thimble, that his friend, Lou Cleary, was working for his son-in-law since his retirement from the force."

"I hope this ain't going to be a long ball," O'Shea says.

Pescaro gives him a look and he shuts up.

I tell them about the request Cleary makes of me to have a talk with Mabel Halstead.

"Used to be Milton Halstead, the cop?" O'Shea asks.

"That's the one. So here's these two cops, off the force, and both in the same line of work," I says, "one of them wanting to talk to the other one about territorial rights and so forth."

"Hold it just a second, there," O'Shea says, tossing a quick look at Pescaro to make sure it's okay for him to stick his oar in and getting the nod.

"You saying there's a possibility here that this woman . . . what did you call her? Fay Wray? . . . could've been under contract to one of these pimps and switched over to the other pimp and the first pimp killed her to teach the rest of his string and his competitor a lesson?"

"I don't think we're dealing with that kind of criminal element here," I says.

"So you don't think it likely that Cleary and Halstead fought over possession and the object of their argument got caught in the middle and trashed?"

I just shake my head. They're in a muddle here. They got two retired cops engaged in illegal and immoral businesses. One of them, a good old boy who's still got ties to other old-timers like Pescaro and these two homicide cops standing right in the room with me, is probably still doing favors for the brass. Providing ladies for birthday parties, smokers and other stag affairs. He's probably got a full bankbook of favors owed to him.

The other cop they got is an embarrassment and a joke, but it don't change the fact that he or she was once one of the blue and deserves at least a benefit of the doubt.

They'd rather not have it be one of them what done the killing, but if one of them didn't do it, that leaves the customer she was servicing the next most likely suspect. And it's pretty clear that they're considering the possibility that Lundatos may have been that client.

Pescaro wanders out of the bedroom, deep in thought, leaving O'Shea behind to keep on poking around.

I follow Pescaro. He sits down, looking thoughtful and tired.

Rourke comes in and says, "Crime Scene on the way."

"That's good," Pescaro says.

"You going to make a call and find out who owns this building?" I asks.

Pescaro looks at Rourke and gives him the nod. Rourke pulls a cellular phone from his pocket, goes over into the corner where he won't bother anybody and dials up.

We sit there, Pescaro and me, old friends, old enemies, men who got a lot of history between us, remembering times when he helped me and other times when I helped him, thinking that here we are again involved in something where I might want to know more about something than people more powerful than us don't want anybody to know.

There's a dead woman in the tub. She sold herself for money. She said she did it because it paid better than working in a shop and lately she did it to take care of a crippled husband. That might not be the whole truth but it's the one she uses to keep herself getting up in the morning.

We sit there until the Mobile Crime Scene crew rings the bell downstairs and O'Shea comes out to buzz them through.

Rourke hangs up after being on the phone all that time.

"I called around," he says. "This building belongs to Twenty-first Century Properties."

"Who the hell owns the company?"

"It's incorporated in the state of Delaware."

"My ass," Pescaro says.

"I got somebody on it," Rourke said, calm and unruffled like he always is, a man growing old, taking one step at a time, never rushing, never losing his temper, except from time to time when he blows off like a howitzer and scares some poor criminal half to death.

"Check the tax rolls," Pescaro says.

Rourke nods and I know he's already started doing that without being told but don't bother saying so.

Eddie Painter, the man from Crime Scene, arrives. He's out of breath.

"The elevator don't work," he says.

"It needs a key," I says.

"Who's got the key? My team ain't going to haul the kit up six flights of stairs. And the boys on the morgue wagon sure as hell ain't going to carry the basket up and down without the elevator."

"If the basket'll fit in the elevator," Pescaro says.

"Sonofabitch," Painter says, a man what is perpetually walking around with a wild hair up his patootie, "we'll stand the fucker up."

18

We're all standing around in the garden room, like we was at a cocktail party, talking about where the key to the elevator could be kept. By the door on a hook? In a cookie jar on the fridge?

"In Fay Wray's purse," I says.

O'Shea gets her purse. Still wearing the rubber gloves, he rummages inside and finds a small ring of keys.

"One of these?" he asks, ready to try the seven or eight possibilities on the ring.

"I'd look for a ring with maybe three keys at the most, what would've been given to Fay Wray some other place, some other time. One for the downstairs door. Maybe another for the elevator and a third one for the door to this flat."

Which is exactly what he finds, three keys on a short piece of braided cord with a little medallion tied to the end of it.

O'Shea checks that it works the front door and then hands it to Painter, who says, "If one of the other two don't open the elevator, somebody's going to have to come down and help us up with the kits."

"For Christ's sake, Painter, go do it. By the time you get around to checking the scene we'll all grow old and retire."

Painter leaves like his nose has been put out of joint. We don't hear from him again until we hear the elevator coming up. Then him and two of his crew come out with all their boxes and go to work, dusting for prints, taking pictures of Fay Wray from every angle, working around us like we wasn't even there and they was hound dogs on the scent.

Then we get a surprise. Who should walk in but Benny Wolper from the State Attorney's Office.

"Well, Benny, what're you doing here?" I asks.

"Benjamin," he says automatically. Every time anybody calls him Benny he corrects them and says his name, because, like he once explained to me, Benny makes it sound like he's still a little kid running around playing stickball in the Fifth Ward on the streets surrounding the University of Chicago where he was brought up.

"So it's you again, is it, Flannery?" he goes on. "What've you got to do with this?"

"Flannery's so clean on this one," O'Shea says, "if you blew in his ear he'd toot."

You could knock me over with a feather, O'Shea coming to my defense that way, except that O'Shea likes Wolper even less than he likes me, so I guess it's a case of the lesser evil.

"Where's the body in question?" Wolper asks.

"Still in the tub," Pescaro says.

"You want to take a peek, get your jollies, Benny?" O'Shea says.

Wolper don't even blink an eyelash, he's good at taking smart remarks. "Benjamin," he says automatically, and goes, making a beeline for the side of the duplex where Fay Wray lays in the tub.

Pescaro and me exchange a glance, thinking the same thing. Wolper's been here before and knows which side of the flat was used for what.

Wolper ain't long.

"You know the lady?" Pescaro asks.

"Yes, as a matter of fact I do," Wolper says. "Her name is Mavis Hovannis."

"How do you spell the last name, Benny?" I asks.

"Benjamin," he mutters, and then tells me it's with two ens.

Pescaro starts asking him where and when he meets Mavis Hovannis, but I ain't interested because I know that Wolper will only tell Pescaro what he wants to tell him. He's over here to put out any fires and to see that none get started. Pescaro's going to get more facts and approximations of the truth than he'll be able to digest. That's Wolper's technique. Pescaro knows it and I know it. But you got to ask the questions and do the job so that some lawyer don't come at you about it some day.

I go looking for a telephone book, which I find in the paneled living room on the shelf of a little telephone stand beside the club chair. Hovannis ain't a common name. There's only two in Chicago.

"You finished with this?" I asks Painter, pointing to the phone.

"It's been checked," he says. "You going to make a call?"

"I was thinking about it."

"Okay, let me make a note. In case it gets dusted again for some reason, I don't want your prints down as an unknown possible suspect."

He grins, which is a rare event.

I dial up the first number in the book, a J. Hovannis, and I get this lady what don't speak English too good.

I ask her is her daughter at home and she keeps asking me something in a language I don't understand until this guy comes on the phone who speaks pretty good English.

"Who dis?" he says.

"This is James Flannery," I says.

"What you want?"

"I'm looking for Mavis Hovannis."

"Who?"

"Does Mavis Hovannis live there?"

"No Hovannis here. Hovaniec."

"Hovaniec?"

"That's right."

"What is the nationality of that name, you don't mind my asking?"

"Bohemian. Is that all you want to know?"

"Do you happen to have a sister named Mavis?"

"Got no sisters," he says, and hangs up.

I hang up and glance over to the door. Pescaro's standing there.

"What're you doing, Flannery?"

"Trying to find out where Mavis Hovannis lives."

"Who was that you were talking to?"

"I didn't get his first name, but he told me his last name wasn't Hovannis, like it is in the telephone book."

"Oh? What did he say it was?"

"Hovaniec."

"Czechoslavokia," Pescaro says. "How many Hovannises in the book?"

"Just two."

"Go ahead, try the other one."

I punch up the second Hovannis. The phone rings five times and I'm about to hang up when an answering machine clicks in and a woman's voice says, "You have reached the home of Mavis and Harry Hovannis. We cannot come to the phone at the moment. Please leave a message at the tone."

I hang up and say, "I got a machine belonging to a Mavis and Harry Hovannis."

Pescaro smiles slightly as though pleased that I struck out twice, or at least got nothing useful out of my two tries.

Wolper comes into the room and stands there like a man with nothing to do.

"You think to look up Fay Wray?" Pescaro asks.

I check the book. There's a listing. I punch up the number. Another machine and message.

"This is Fay Wray. I cannot come to the phone at the moment. Please leave a message or if you wish, you may dial my beeper."

But she leaves no beeper number on the message.

I give the news to Pescaro, who smiles wider than before.

"Give me the phone," he says. He dials the operator, asks for the reverse directory, gives his police identification and tells the operator the number I just dialed.

"Remember this address, Flannery. We'll go over there and knock on the door. Seven nineteen Fullerton."

"You're asking me to go along?"

"I want you to know what I know when I get to know it, Flannery. I don't want anybody yelling police cover-up on this one."

"Where are you going?" Wolper asks.

"You want to be part of this investigation, too?" Pescaro asks good-naturedly. "You want to do some legwork, too, so you can say you helped the cops in their investigation?"

Wolper flushes and waves his hands as though dismissing not only what Pescaro just said, but what he didn't say, which could be did Wolper want to tag along to try and put a damper on whatever evidence showed up that could implicate his client, whoever that client, at the moment, might be.

The morgue men arrive with the folding stretcher and a plastic body bag, no wicker basket here.

"We don't got to wait, Jimmy," Pescaro says, switching from the bland impersonal Flannery to the friendly warm personal Jimmy. "O'Shea and Rourke can do what more has to be done here."

I wonder if this is just more of the honey cake I been getting from Pescaro ever since I became a ward leader. If that's the case, I wonder what courtesies I can expect if I do team up with Lundatos, with the aldermanic seat of the Eleventh in my future.

19

Harry and Mavis Hovannis live on the first floor of a three-flat on Fullerton, in the Thirtieth Ward, just down the street from Hanson Stadium, which is the only stadium in Chicago not used by a major college or professional sports team.

Ted Gabinski's the Democratic committeeman and his wife, Doris Gabinski, is the alderman, both of whom I know good enough to ask how's the family but not good enough to get an answer back much more than okay, thanks for asking.

The neighborhood is known as Belmont Cragin and don't boast much except factories like the Helene Curtis cosmetic plant and the Archer-Daniels-Midland grain elevator. Naming such landmarks is always dangerous and you could be corrected because one or more has went out of business since last you looked. Just like when the W. F. Hall printing plant at Diversey and Kenton left the city in the middle of the eighties.

There's plenty of Irish pubs, in fact there's one right at the corner, and a lot of Puerto Rican stores, bars and fast-food restaurants but the streets and houses don't look particularly ethnic. Just a lot of plain everyday housing for the workers that you'll see in any factory town, the factory owners and bosses living elsewhere.

The entrance into the foyer is level with the sidewalk, easy access for a man in a wheelchair.

There ain't no reason to ring the bell on the mailbox in the vestibule because the inside front door's open.

"You want to give him notice?" I asks.

"You called. We gave him notice," Pescaro says.

I don't like what we're going to have to do and I'm sorry I agreed to come along.

We go to the door beside the stairway and knock on the flimsy paneling.

Two minutes later, there's no answer, not even anybody yelling to wait a minute.

"Maybe we should've kept on calling until we got him home," I says.

"The man's supposed to be in a wheelchair, didn't you say? The man's supposed to not be able to go anywhere without his wife, didn't you tell me?"

"Maybe he's lying down in a bedroom at the back," I says.

We walk down the cold, gloomy hallway, which smells of cabbage a hundred years old, and knock on the pebbled pane of glass set in what is probably the kitchen door. Again we wait. Just as we're about to give it up a muffled voice says, "Who is it and what do you want?"

"Mr. Hovannis?" Pescaro says, raising his voice.

"Yeah?"

"Police. We've got something to tell you, Mr. Hovannis."

There's some noise behind the door and when it gets pulled open, there's a man about fifty sitting in a wheelchair with a light blanket covering his knees and legs. He's sweating even though he's wearing a sleeveless underwear shirt and the kitchen's no warmer than the hallway.

His upper body is the body of a weight lifter, maybe

from pushing the wheels on the chair all the time, and lifting himself up on couches and the bed.

He's a good-looking guy except that his complexion's sallow like he ain't been getting much sun. There's pale freckles on his shoulders, chest and upper arms. He's in a neck brace. His eyes are scared.

"Something's happened to Mavis," he says, making it a statement, not a question.

"What makes you say that?" Pescaro asks, which, under the circumstances, I think is a little cruel.

"When cops come to the door, it's usually bad news."

"I'm afraid you read it right," Pescaro says.

"Did somebody beat her up?"

"What makes you say that?" Pescaro says again.

Hovannis scowls. He looks like an angry turtle.

"You think I don't know what she does to support me?" Hovannis asks, like somebody was sticking a knife in him. "How bad did the sonofabitch hurt her?"

"As bad as it gets," I says, before Pescaro can carry on the way he's carrying on.

Hovannis closes his eyes real slow and sits like that. Tears come out of his eyes and run down the lines of his cheeks into the corners of his mouth.

"You all right, Mr. Hovannis?" Pescaro asks.

"No, I ain't all right," Hovannis says. "Is that all you got to say to me?"

"The law requires an eyewitness identification," Pescaro says.

"Where?"

"The morgue."

"When?"

"Whenever you say."

"The sooner the better."

"I'll send a van inside the hour. You'll be here?"

"I ain't going anywhere," Hovannis says.

We leave. When we're outside I asks Pescaro why he was so rough on the man.

"A woman dies, suspect the man closest to her, husband, father or lover," Pescaro says.

"For Christ's sake, the man's a cripple."

"They got upper-body strength."

"What'd he do, push his chair up six flights of stairs?"

"She could've let him in. She could've sent the elevator down for him."

"If that's the case," I says, "I don't think you'll have much trouble finding witnesses to a man in a neck brace and wheelchair rolling away from the scene of a murder."

Pescaro stops and gives me the old one-eye.

"So I'm a sonofabitch, Flannery. It goes with the job."

20

Pescaro leaves me at the morgue to walk . . . or push . . . Hovannis through the identification.

Chicago works it like most cities work it nowadays. It ain't like in the movies or on television where the friend or relatives stands there while a morgue attendant pulls out a drawer and whips back a sheet.

How it works is, the body's not even in the room. It's in another room altogether and the person identifying it is elsewhere looking at closed-circuit television.

So this is one way that we keep on getting some distance between ourselves and some of the harder things in life, which may not be altogether a good thing.

As it happens, Hovannis don't want to see a picture of his dead wife. He not only wants to be in the room with her but when I wheel him in there, he wants to touch her.

Eddie Ferguson gives me a look when Hovannis pushes aside the sheet and takes her hand, his head held in this neck brace which ain't one of them things with Velcro closures that you wear for maybe a week or two when you twist your neck or suffer a minor backlash.

It's a terrible device. Something you'd deliberately inflict on somebody to torture them.

I got to turn away from seeing the struggle it is for him to get a good look at his dead wife's face.

"Help me," he says.

Eddie and me get on either side of him and lift him out of the wheelchair and hold him on his feet, bent over so he can stare down at her.

"Get me closer," he says.

It ain't easy but we manage to get him positioned so he can kiss her on the corner of the mouth. He's crying.

"Ah, God, babe, I told you to leave the goddamn life," he says. "I told you not to have anything to do with that bastard."

He sort of slumps and puts his forehead on her breast. Eddie and me almost lose our grip on him.

We get him back in the chair.

"Can you make the identification, sir?" Eddie asks.

I give him a look.

"I'm sorry, Jimmy, but I got to hear him say it for the affidavit here."

"What do you want me to say? I, Harry Hovannis, husband of Mavis Hovannis, declare and avow that this is her and she is dead?"

He's being sarcastic, even behind his grief, like people get, as though all the clerks and pencil pushers they got to deal with at times like these is to blame.

I put my hand on his shoulder. It's trembling.

"You okay?" I asks.

When he don't say anything, I wheel him out of the room, leaving Fay Wray there for what comes next.

The cop what drove Hovannis over in a van rigged for wheelchair access is waiting out in the lobby. I turn Hovannis over to him.

"Can I ask you one more question, Mr. Hovannis?"

"Anything I can say to stop you?"

"Who was the bastard you told your wife not to see?"

He almost blurts it out, but something stops him and he gets sly. "I'll tell you when I decide what to do about it," he says.

"I hope what you decide to do ain't anything foolish, like confronting this person and making threats," I says.

He turns his whole head and shoulders away from me, telling me in no uncertain terms that the conversation is over.

"Anything I can do, Mr. Hovannis, don't hesitate to ask," I says.

He holds up his hand but still don't say anything and the cop wheels him out.

"Hackman around?" I asks Eddie.

"In his office, I think," he says.

"Thanks for everything," I says.

"How come you witnessed the identification?" he asks.

"I think Pescaro wants me to see what it's like doing what a cop's got to do."

Hackman's in his office all right, leaning back in an old-fashioned wooden swivel chair, his feet up on the desk, sleeping, a dead cigar in his mouth.

He's one of those people who wakes up and is instantly alert. His eyes pop open and he says, "You're here about the woman found in the tub."

"That's right," I says.

"Broken neck," he says.

"Did somebody break it for her?"

"That I couldn't tell you. It looks like she might've slipped getting into the tub and hit the edge with her jaw as she went down. She may have tried to turn around and sit up but couldn't. Went unconscious and slumped down just far enough to cover her nose and mouth."

"Drowned in six inches of water without anybody holding her down?"

"It happens."

"Choked to death without a struggle?"

"How do you know it was without a struggle?" he asks.

"Because the floor was dry."

"You ever hear of evaporation?"

"The water in the tub was still warm. I don't think there was enough time for a wet floor to dry," I says.

"I didn't say it couldn't have been a punch in the jaw that knocked her out and even broke her neck," he says.

"That going to be in your report?"

"Of course not. I don't speculate about such things in my reports. I just lay down the physical evidence."

"Are you going to do an autopsy?"

"You mean split her down the middle and saw off the top of her head?"

I maybe wince because he reaches over like he's going to pat me.

"Take it easy," he says. "She a friend of yours?"

"I only met her once."

"Was it a special meeting?"

I understand what he's saying. He's been told by somebody that Mavis Hovannis aka Fay Wray was a companion for hire. I wonder who told him. I know if I ask, he won't say.

"It was after Delvin's funeral."

"I forget how people feel about autopsies sometimes," he says. "When there's no special reason to suspect poison or other subtle means of death, I've got no reason to do anything but a basic postmortem on her unless somebody orders it. You think I should do more?"

"I don't know what to think," I says. "You take any swabs?"

"The usual."

"There was semen?"

"What would you expect considering the woman's line of work?"

"I'd expect her to make the customer wear a condom," I says.

"You'd be surprised how many don't. They're half-drunk or half-stoned or too tired to face an argument or they just forget it," he says.

"We're not talking about streetwalkers or bar girls here," I says. "We're talking about a very high-class professional. I don't think she'd forget to make a customer wear a skin anymore than she'd forget to brush her teeth."

"All right, if you believe that, what does it tell you?"

"It tells me that the client must've been a very special customer, indeed."

"So run with it," he says.

"You're saving samples for future serology and DNA tests?" I asks.

He nods. "What are you doing in this anyway?" he asks.

"I got a phone call. I was the first one on the scene . . . except whoever made the call."

"But how do you come to be acting like a cop?"

"Pescaro hands me the package," I says. "He needs a witness that everything was done right. He made me the witness."

Hackman smiles. "I see his point. You can't go yelling cover-up if you been in on it from the beginning and walk it through all the way."

I shake Hackman's hand, thank him for the news and take my leave.

On the way home I'm thinking about how the sequence could've gone.

Fay Wray services the client in the love nest. He leaves because he may have a wife to go home to. She stays behind and sleeps over, taking a rest from all the care she's got to give her husband night after night.

In the morning she gets up and goes into the bathroom to have a bath.

Somebody, maybe the customer, has gained entrance to the flat. He confronts her just as she's about to step into the tub. There's a quarrel or maybe he does what he comes to do without even exchanging words.

Or she knows this john is coming back in the morning

for another taste. She runs herself a bath, getting ready for
him . . . this ain't no fifty-dollar trick. She steps into the
bath. She slips and twists around trying to save herself from
a bad tumble, but she goes right on over and smacks her
jaw against the side of the tub and she's down and under.
She never comes to.

The customer arrives and finds her. He calls me.

Why the hell does he call me?

And who buzzed me in, then ran away from the flat?

You can see where I am. I'm nowhere.

21

I'm wore out from the emotional stress and running around.

I go back to Bridgeport to the house where my old Chinaman used to live not long ago and I'm hit all over again with a sense of loss.

The door's open to let the dust out. I walk into the entry hall and it ain't anything like it was. All the pictures celebrating Delvin's life, the political rallies, the picnics, the testimonial dinners for the Democratic Central Committee and the Sons of Hibernia, is all down, neatly filed away in cardboard boxes lined up on the floor.

The house smells fresh and clean, a little bit like lemon oil, a little bit like pine-scented cleaner.

I could cry.

I stoop down so I can finger through some of the old sepia photos.

Mary steps into the doorway to the living room. I look up. She's in jeans and a cotton blouse tied around her middle just under her breasts. There's a bandana tied around her hair.

"I wasn't going to throw any of them out before consulting you, James," she says.

"Throw them away?"

"I mean give them to some historical society or the new library. Somebody who'd want them and would know what to do with them."

"There's a few I'd like to keep. Hang back up on the wall. Maybe not here in the hall, but someplace."

"There's plenty of room," Mary says. "I picked out a room downstairs, the old sunporch, for your office. It's got walnut paneling and an old mahogany desk that'll clean up beautifully. A few of those old photos in new frames would look very impressive."

"Impressive?"

"Pictures like those on the wall will assure your constituents of the continuity you mean to bring to the ward."

"Constituents?"

I'm talking to her like I'm some dim-witted gazooney without a thought in his head.

"I mean, if you run for committeeman alongside Lundatos, you could have your office right at home. There's a separate entrance."

"Delvin ran the Twenty-seventh but he lived here in the Eleventh," I says. "I don't know what continuity you're talking about."

"Of tradition, James."

I stand up, feeling a little creaky.

"You look tired," Mary says.

"You don't," I says. "I don't understand it. You been moving things around and cleaning this house since seven o'clock this morning and you look fresh as a daisy."

She colors with pleasure a little bit. She ain't lost that even after we been married now . . . what . . . nine years, going on ten. She still blushes when I give her a compliment.

"Mary?" Aunt Sada calls from somewhere upstairs.

"I've had help," Mary says. "Go look around. There's

still lots to do. You want to have a yard sale or would you rather give whatever we can't use away to some charity?"

"Let me think about it," I says. "Maybe we can offer it around to individuals what ain't got, as long as we can make it so it don't look like we're buying votes."

"You and Lundatos?"

"We'll see."

She climbs the stairs after Sada calls again and I go into the living room.

The old worn carpets are off the floor, rolled up against the wall. The dusty lace curtains and heavy brocade drapes are down.

Stanley Recore, the kid what used to talk so funny when he was small, is up on a stepladder washing the tall windows. I notice he's got what you might call the hope of a mustache on his upper lip.

He stares at me, which I realize is about all I been getting from him the last couple years. We ain't enemies but we sure ain't pals like we used to be when he'd come busting in on me, and sometimes Mary and me, unannounced, having a talent with locks that would make a housebreaker green with envy.

"How's it going?" I says.

"It's going," he says.

"I ain't seen you around much lately," I says.

"I ain't been around much lately," he says.

I wave my hand, telling him to go ahead with what he's doing if he wants to. He don't wait for a second invitation but goes right back to work.

Mary, Sada and Stanley have shoved all the furniture back against the walls. In the light of day they look worn. The couch has sprung some springs and the stuffing's coming out of the upholstery, which is that mohair I ain't seen in thirty years. Even Delvin's favorite easy chair, the one from which he gives me a thousand years of experience and good advice, the one made of leather, is so cracked that there's no way of saving it.

The end tables are rickety and the coffee table scarred and stained, maybe beyond repair. The glass-fronted book-cases look dusty but otherwise okay.

I catch myself and stop what I'm doing, taking a god-damn inventory of an old friend's belongings.

I wander back through the house.

There's an office off the hall that nobody's got to yet, with a rolltop desk and a wooden swivel chair. There's even a spittoon on the floor, which I suppose is Delvin's idea of interior decorating, and more pictures on the wall, including a big framed print of Chicago back in 1912.

One of the three windows is made of stained glass. It shows a man in armor on horseback fighting a dragon with a spear. I suppose it's Saint George, though what Saint George, an Englishman, has got to do with Delvin escapes me.

The next room down the hall is a bathroom. I can see it's going to cost a little money bringing it up to date.

And right across the hall is the bedroom where Delvin breathed his last.

The kitchen's at the end. It's big and bright with all the curtains and shades down. There's a big pantry, what used to be called a larder, right there. There's not much by way of canned goods and staples on the shelves. I guess old Delvin and Mrs. Thimble didn't eat so much that they needed to stock up for themselves and I doubt he'd had a dinner guest since his wife passed away.

There's a porch off the kitchen, part of it glassed off. What they call a sunporch. The place where I'm supposed to hold office hours when I get to be the committeeman of the Eleventh.

I go wandering back through the house and up the stairs.

My wife and Sada and my mother-in-law and Gloria Chapman, all dressed for housework, are in the master bed-room, which is twice as big as the one we got at home.

They all look at me like I'm going to say something.

"This ain't the room he died in," I says.

"He wouldn't have been sleeping in here," Sada says. "All the stairs at his age."

"Where's Mrs. Thimble?"

"I saw her this morning when I arrived," Mary says. "She said she had errands to run."

"She didn't want to be in the way," I says.

"I think she's getting ready for a trip," Sada says. "She said something about arranging for a flight to Texas."

"Oh, yes, she's got relatives there. Is she coming back?"

"I suppose she will," Charlotte says. "All her clothes and things are still in her room across the hall."

"Are you all right, James?" Mary says.

"You remember a nice-looking woman at the funeral feast—"

"You mean the one you took out to the backyard for a chat?" I'm not surprised Mary noticed that and I ain't surprised she never mentioned it until I just brought it up. "The one who introduced herself as Fay Wray?"

Sada makes a sound through her nose to let us know what she thinks of that.

"Well, I got a call this morning to go over to a three-flat conversion a couple of blocks from here."

"From Fay Wray?" Sada asks.

"From a man who didn't identify hisself," I says. "But Fay Wray . . . her real name's Mavis Hovannis . . . was there. Dead. Drowned in the bathtub."

They just stand there, turned to stone. Nobody even asks was it homicide or death by misadventure.

22

There's nothing any of my ladies can do about a dead call girl.

That don't sound right to my inner ear and it makes me stop and think about it for a minute. This business about making women into children, the better to push them around. Here's a female selling sex, which many men got a great need for, and the men feel it necessary to call them girls so they won't be so intimidated about buying the use of another person's body.

Mary asks me how I'm feeling. Do I want her to come home with me?

"You still got plenty to do here and it wouldn't be right for you to leave with all these helping hands," I says.

"You want to break for supper?" she asks. "We were going to send Mike out for Italian or Chinese takeout."

"Where is he?"

"Getting some cleaning supplies. We ran out of some things. So you want to stay for Chinese?"

"I think I should be getting home," I says. "I have an

idea somebody or other's going to be trying to contact me. I'll get something on the way."

"No corned beef on rye," Mary says.

"Nothing like that. Maybe a slice of quiche," I says, and give her a grin. "What about Kathleen? Was you planning for me to pick her up and take her home with me?"

"I was, but if you're expecting a call, you might have to go out again. Mom or Aunt Sada will go pick her up and bring her back here."

So we got on like that, setting up all the little trips and chores and sharing like married people do, making sure the other person is okay about the way things are sorting themselves out.

"What time do you expect to be home tonight?" I asks.

"No later than nine or ten," she says.

"You'll never get it all done."

"I never expected to. Mom, Mike and Sada are going to stay here tonight instead of driving all the way back to Mount Pleasant, but I'll be coming home. I don't want to take a chance of Kathleen getting upset. Gloria'll drive us home, so don't you worry if you have to go out."

"Gloria coming over tomorrow?"

"She can't, but she's already done the work of three."

"I'll go thank her."

"You're antsy about getting out of here and back home," she says. "I can tell. I'll do all the thanking that's necessary."

"So, okay," I says, standing there feeling awkward and not knowing why, except that I'm already feeling like I'm without a home, being neither here or there.

"I'll come back with you tomorrow and give you a hand," I says.

"Don't you worry," Mary says, "there'll be plenty to do for the next year or so."

"I'm looking forward to it," I says.

She comes over and gives me a kiss. "It ain't going to be so tough, babe," she says.

*   *   *

The phone's ringing the minute I walk through the door.

I pick up and hardly before I can say hello, this guys says, "Flannery?"

"Who am I talking to?" I asks.

"Johnny O'Meara hisself."

"What can I do for you, Mr. O'Meara?"

"Johnny. Call me Johnny. All right if I call you Jimmy?"

"Practically everybody does."

"Well, practically nobody calls me Johnny. Only my closest friends and colleagues."

"Well, thank you, Johnny," I says.

"I understand a mutual friend made you a political proposition."

"I only got one proposition, political or otherwise, lately, so I assume we're talking about the same mutual friend."

"You'll understand my reluctance to bandy his name about on the telephone."

No, I don't understand his reluctance except that old pols like O'Meara got a natural disinclination to use names in any conversation that can be overheard or over any device that can be tapped.

"I was wondering if it was too late in the evening for us to get together and chew the fat for a little while," he goes on.

"How long you think it'll take?" I asks.

"Depends," he says, which is the kind of answer you can always expect from a politician. Everything depends. Options always open. No promises made that can't be avoided, delayed, denied or reneged on.

"I think I can talk for an hour or so," I says.

"That should be plenty. Hey, I understand you and your old man is a fan of kielbasa and cabbage."

"We enjoy a dish now and then."

"At a certain establishment we all know."

He's talking about Dan Blatna's Last Chance Saloon over to the Thirty-fourth, where, before I was married, me

and my old man used to have a plate practically every
Wednesday.

"So how about meeting there as soon as you can make
it?" he says, and then hangs up before I can reply.

Even though Mary knows I could be out when she gets
home, I leave a note anyway.

And I drive over to Dan Blatna's.

It's crowded in the Last Chance, it being Saturday night
and half of Chicago out having a meal and a chance to
enjoy rubbing elbows with all the strangers they hate rubbing elbows with the rest of the week.

You could cut the smoke with a knife, the ban on smoking in restaurants you read about elsewhere in the country
not having reached the heartland of the country.

But, even packed as it is, there's a table in a little bend of
the room near the kitchen, blocked off by a panel of etched
and frosted glass, what is kept for people doing business.
It's like an oasis of quiet at the edge of a rushing river.
There's not an old tavern or restaurant in Chicago what
ain't got a similar arrangement.

I start walking back toward it and as I get closer I can
count the heads at the big table.

There's O'Meara, a big, unlit cigar in his freckled mitt,
and Smith Jarwolski, the superintendent of police, wearing
a pinstripe three-piece suit worth maybe two grand.

Ray Carrigan, still the Cook County Democratic Party
leader, is head-to-head with Harlan Shanker, this young,
maybe thirty-five-year-old, lawyer from the State Attorney's Office, who everybody says is going to climb the ladder of power like a cat scrambling up a tree.

I met him once or twice, here and there. He's got a grin
like a cat, that never gets to his eyes, which are the coldest
and meanest I ever see except in the head of this serial
killer who murdered twelve girls and boys over to Cicero.

So that's four and Lundatos makes five.

The sixth head belongs to a very handsome older

woman, I'd say maybe fifty-five, sixty, but it's hard to say. Not that she's made up trying to look young, but because she's got these bones and skin like milk with some girlish freckles across the bridge of her nose and the bluest eyes I ever see. There's a slash of hot-pink lipstick on her mouth, just on the edge of looking slutty, and hair, streaked with gray, combed in a style halfway between windblown and regal.

She's got this way of sitting there, like she's there but she's not there.

I probably never would've noticed all these little signs before I started living with my wife, Mary, and met up with Janet Canarias, probably the most beautiful lipstick lesbian in Chicago, alderman of the Twenty-seventh and my political confidante in many matters.

I watch how Janet uses her femininity and her looks to work the crowd and give herself an edge.

I remember once me and her and Mabel Halstead, who used to be Milton, the cop, having a strategy session over coffee in the alderman's storefront headquarters. I don't remember what the problem was, but Janet was going to meet with some very important people in three days. It's summer and she's wearing this man-tailored, two-piece foam-colored suit with a midcalf-length skirt what was slit almost up to her panty line. Mabel asks her is that the outfit she's going to wear to the meeting and Janet sticks out her long leg so the skirt opens up and falls back and gives us a look at her thigh and says, "You bet your sweet ass. I'm going to use everything I got."

So what you got to remember, maybe more with women than with men, because they got more tricks, like makeup, clothes and a man's natural inclination to go brain-dead around a sexually powerful woman, is that a lot of what you see is illusion and it's only when what you see and what you get matches up that you got a shot at something very good.

Smith Jarwolski's the first to see me coming, but he

don't say anything and don't smile, me and Jarwolski not being exactly what you'd call the best of friends, having tangled horns from time to time.

Shanker, looking lazy and relaxed but missing nothing, like a lizard on a rock, cuts his eyes in my direction, but he don't get up to take my hand or nothing either.

The lady's looking at me, too. She gets this little smile on her lips like she's amused to see me. Like she's already fond of me though we've never met.

Then Carrigan glances in my direction, drawn to me because of the way the other three are looking at me. All of a sudden I feel like I'm under the gun. Like I could make a serious mistake if I ain't careful.

He grabs the napkin off his lap with one hand and starts to stand up, though he's half-pinned to his seat by Jarwolski on one side and the lady on the other.

O'Meara's up and walking the two or three steps I still got to go. He's the first to speak.

"Ah, there you are, Jimmy, my boy. We been waiting on you."

The honey's dripping off me from his tone of voice, his big smile and his handshake.

Then they're up one after another, in the polite half-crouch of people greeting people in restaurants.

Except for Lundatos and the lady sitting next to him.

I ain't surprised when he introduces her as his wife, Margaret, holding onto my hand a little bit longer than a shake should take, getting my attention, telling me he feels good about me. If he had the room, he would've give me the old Lyndon Johnson two-hander, which has become a favorite of politicians and undertakers all over the country.

"Will you have a whiskey?" O'Meara's asking.

And all three, Lundatos, Jarwolski and Shanker, says, "Don't you know Flannery don't touch the stuff?" one way or another.

Where Shanker got that news I'd surely like to know. He could be one of them people who's a vacuum cleaner, sucking up and remembering every little bit of news that comes his way, or it could mean he's made a special effort to find out about me.

"What shall I call you, Mr. Flannery?" Margaret Lundatos says, like she expects we're going to be old friends before the night is over.

"Ginger ale," I says to O'Meara. "You can call me Jim or Jimmy, if you like," I says to her. "I answer to either and both."

"And you may call me Peg or Maggie, Jim," she says right back. It's a little thing . . . I don't know how many other people would even notice it . . . but we just made a declaration that we expected to treat each other special. We just cut a deal to be honest with one another, balancing frankness with previous obligations, and that was all right with me.

I take one of the two empty chairs at the table.

The waiter comes over with my glass of ginger ale, O'Meara having given him the order when me and Maggie was otherwise occupied. Now he orders fresh drinks for everybody else and tells the waiter to take the miniature cabbage rolls and baby sausages away and bring hot.

"Well, Jimmy," O'Meara says, "we were hoping you'd have an answer for us about the offer the congressman give you the other day."

"I think there's something else come up more important to the congressman—"

"Leo," Lundatos tosses in, like a stone in a pond, knowing that whenever he wants to interrupt, everybody else is going to shut up until he's said his piece, even if it's only one word. One word what makes ripples of silence until the talk goes on.

In that minute I understand a little bit about the nature of power and the pecking order than I ever took a good look at before.

At the table here it's Lundatos, then Carrigan, then Shanker, then Jarwolski and finally O'Meara.

Maggie and me are wild cards, neither of use having bought into everyone else's estimation of themselves. So, in a way, we can set the agenda, if we want to.

"Leo. Thank you," I says.

"You were going to say something more important than whether or not you and me run as a team in the Eleventh?" he says.

"I'd say so."

"What makes you say that?"

"Because of the group you've got assembled here."

"Just my darling wife and a few close friends who might be my principal advisers if I announce my candidacy."

"You don't need a top cop, a top prosecutor and the top county Democrat to do that."

He's looking at me with this fixed smile on his face like a doctor who just heard you diagnose your own case of appendicitis or diabetes and wants to hear you tell him how you got the information to make such a fool of yourself.

"Then why do you think they're here?"

I take a swallow of my ginger ale to think about how far I want to commit myself here, just to prove what a smart guy I am, staring at the red dot of a maraschino cherry in my glass.

"May I have your cherry?" Maggie says, reaching out with her slender fingers to pluck it out by the stem before I can say yes or no, knowing that I certainly ain't going to say no. "I'm a sucker for these things even though they're dyed with chemicals that are undoubtedly bad for me."

She's telling me to bite the bullet. Take my chances. Go with my instincts. Do the triple without a net.

"Because they can tell you the extent of your liability and involvement in the matter of a woman found dead in a building on Lowe over to Bridgeport."

Now it's his turn to think things over, but he don't break eye contact while he makes up his mind.

"I don't own the building," Lundatos says. "I don't even know about any such building until my wife brings me the word that a woman was found drowned in a luxury flat over in Bridgeport. On Lowe, you say?"

"You don't mind my asking," I says, "how come the authorities bring you the news about a homicide in a luxury flat in a building you don't own or know anything about? How come you call me down here for a power drink and tell me I've got no interest in the death of Fay Wray?"

"Because I don't want my running mate calling down public scrutiny and media speculation on us," he says.

"We got enough of that, right?"

"Don't cut your throat for a one-liner, Jimmy," O'Meara says.

The others just glare at me.

Lundatos is walking a wire here. On the one hand he wants to reassure me that his skirts are clean. On the other hand he's got to assert his power, making it clear to me that he's the king of the jungle and I'm nothing but another jackal running with the pack. On the third hand he wants to flatter me and let me know he considers me a cut above the rest.

"Let's stop avoiding the issue," Maggie suddenly says, looking at me but talking to her husband. "If we intend to solicit Jim's discretion in this matter, don't you all think it would be wise to put the cards on the table?"

They're all a little bit shocked, straightforward not being their normal method of operation.

O'Meara's the first to recover. "Right as ever, dear lady," he coos.

She tosses him a sweet sidelong glance that could take the hide off an alligator without drawing blood.

"The building in which the unfortunate woman was found dead belongs to me," Maggie says. "The deed is held in trust by Twenty-first Century Properties, filed under the trusteeship of Higgens, Huggins and Burke. Higgens and Huggins were cousins of mine, since gone to their reward, and Burke is me. I was briefly married to Charlie Burke . . . you know Charlie Burke?"

"I heard of Charlie Burke," I says. "Real estate developer. He's dead and gone these fifteen years, ain't he?"

"He was a lot older than I when we married. He was a friend of my Uncle's Joe's. It was a schoolgirl crush for me. I expect it was a good deal more for Charlie, but I couldn't know that back then. I wasn't smart enough. I thought that all he wanted was a hard body and a trophy wife. Young women understand more about that than you might imagine, but very little about genuine feelings. After a year or two, I got to feeling that I was nothing but an old rich man's toy and that wasn't good enough for me. He agreed to a divorce. He gave me the company he'd set up with my cousins as a conduit for several real estate deals. There were a couple of properties left in it. That was my settlement, provided that I wouldn't revert to my maiden name or change my name until I remarried. I think he just wanted everyone to know that he'd owned me once, as if anybody outside the circle of his immediate friends would care. I met Leo five years later and then, of course, I did change my name."

I think I know what she's getting at here, but I don't interrupt. I just sit there listening while she tells me her story.

"My maiden name was Cooley. If anybody becomes interested in the ownership of that building they'll get to Twenty-first Century and probably to Higgens, Huggins and Burke but I doubt they'll every get to Margaret Cooley."

"Are you getting an idea of what's wanted here?" Shanker says, taking it upon hisself to stick his oar into waters where it ain't been invited to be.

I don't give him the courtesy of an answer.

He's there, I think, acting as the deputy for the State Attorney's Office, and he ain't supposed to be asking questions or making comments, but he just can't resist.

Lundatos coughs and Maggie smiles at Shanker like he was a puppy who peed on the rug. The others are vaguely embarrassed in one of them odd moments when somebody does something stupid and everybody takes the blame onto themselves.

Maggie turns them blue eyes back to me.

"Some especially energetic and industrious reporter might dig up the connection but I don't see why one would. An expensive call girl was found dead, because of an unfortunate accident, in the bathroom of a luxury flat in the Eleventh Ward, home of Chicago mayors. You must take my word that Leo knew nothing about my ownership of that building. I'm afraid that a couple of the things Burke taught me, in the brief time we were married, was always have a hidden stash and never let your right hand know what your left hand's doing."

She reaches out to take her husband's hand then, like she's asking his forgiveness for the secrets kept from him. It looks like she's done with explanations and pleas.

"So you want me to join up in a conspiracy to keep it quiet," I says, finally answering Shanker's question about do I know what's wanted here.

"Are you going to give us one of your holy howls claiming official cover-up?" Jarwolski says, in this voice meant to challenge me and make me sound a fool at the same time.

"It ain't only me that howls, Superintendent," I says. "You know as good as me that some things can't be covered up, though you people keep on trying. 'Murder will out,' somebody said, and this could be murder. It's going to come out no matter how you scramble to throw a blanket over it."

"We're pretty sure we can cover them," O'Meara says, all of a sudden the wise old counselor instead of the brash glad-hander.

"Do you know how many people got to be told to shut their mouths?" I says. "There's the boys from the Mobile Crime Scene crew, the people down in the Coroner's Office and the homicide cops—"

"All of whom catch two or three of these call girls

killings a month. If nobody else officially takes special notice it goes into the files as a homicide committed by a person or persons unknown. It's forgotten in a week. It's like it never happened in a month," Jarwolski says.

"And when Leo runs for alderman and they start looking for dirt on his shoes and soot on his fingers?"

"You think the whole world lives politics like you and me?" O'Meara asks. "Well, they don't give a rat's ass most of the time. That's why you got forty-two percent of forty percent of the voting age population electing a president."

"There's the people what maintain the building. Rumors fly. There's the pizza man and the guy what brings the laundry."

Jarwolski, O'Meara and Lundatos shake their heads, making me feel like I'm just picking things out of the air.

"We're talking about a dead whore, here," Jarwolski says.

"There's one person you forgot?" I says.

"Who might that be?" Margaret asks.

"The man what called me on the telephone and got me over to that building. The man suggested that Leo might have something to say about what I find there. The man who wasn't there when I got there, but is still out there somewhere."

"That's being taken care of," Shanker says, and this time nobody acts like he spilled his drink. "Trust us on this."

"We're not asking you to do anything," O'Meara says. "We're asking you to just *not* do anything."

"Well?" somebody practically whispers.

I don't even know who says it or if anybody says it, but I just think somebody says it, because I know it's the question on everybody's mind. Am I going to go along? Am I going to run as a team with Lundatos, who'll serve a term and then turn the alderman's seat over to me? Have I had a taste of power by becoming warlord of the Twenty-seventh and can I withstand the pull of ambition? Will I go along to get along?

They say they got the bases covered pretty good, though I don't want to think about what Shanker means when he says they got the problem of the anonymous caller covered. I'm the loose cannon who could maybe sink the ship.

Another glass of ginger ale appears in front of me, with a maraschino cherry glowing like a tiny stoplight on top of the ice.

"Well?" I hear again.

This time I know somebody said it because I see Lundatos's lips move.

I notice he's squeezing his wineglass like he's holding hisself back from smacking me in the face.

"I got to have a little time to think," I hear myself saying.

His wineglass breaks. I pull out my clean pocket handkerchief and hand it to him as Maggie makes noises of concern. She wraps my handkerchief around his hand.

"For Christ's sake, Flannery," Lundatos says.

I knew it was the wrong thing to say when I said it. They give me the facts. They made the offer. Sleeping on them is a sign of weakness to these people. They want a decision and I ain't giving it to them.

"Sleep on it, Flannery," Jarwolski says. "Do that. Think about who'll be there to listen if you decide to spill your guts."

"Think about what you really got to say, Jimmy," O'Meara says, his tongue dripping honey again. "You got a call from a man that wasn't there. What was you doing going to a flat in the Eleventh? Why, you hardly get out of the Twenty-seventh for more than an hour nowadays. Why was you going to a flat in which a professional lady, who you had a rendezvous with at Delvin's funeral feast, was waiting?"

"Don't threaten Mr. Flannery," Maggie says. We look at one another. She smiles.

I'll tell you the truth, if I wasn't married with a child, both of who I dearly love, and even taking into account what other people might think was an unsuitable difference in our ages, and if, of course, she was willing, I wouldn't think twice about having a relationship with Margaret Cooley Burke Lundatos.

"Think about my husband's offer," she says, like being her husband's running mate is all we've been talking about.

"I'll do that," I says.

Lundatos unwraps his hand and looks at the cut. It ain't bleeding any more.

Maggie reaches for the handkerchief. "I'll see that it's washed and returned to you," she says.

I take it from her fingers.

"No, no," I says, letting them know that, at the moment, I won't even accept that small courtesy.

23

I drive past the fancy conversion on Lowe on the way past the new house on the way to the old flat.

I just heard Maggie Lundatos take a shot at getting her husband off the hook and shut up a person . . . me . . . what is known for sticking his nose in where a lot of people don't think it belongs.

I've got no reason to believe she didn't tell me the truth except that she's a wife and a political wife to boot, which means telling lies is only bad or good depending on reasons and results.

I stop at a telephone booth and ring up the number of this bar and grill what takes this friend Willy Dink's messages.

Willy Dink is an exterminator of rare and unusual talents. He don't use chemicals, poisons or sprays. You got ants, he brings in a small armadillo. You got mice in the walls, he brings in a snake and a ferret. You got rats, he's got this little terrier by the name of Timmy.

Willy Dink lives in a truck with a wooden camper body he built hisself. A very nice sign he's painted on the side says "Willy Dink's Natural Vermin Control" with, under it, this coat of arms which is made up of a mailed fist, a snake, a ferret, and a terrier and a ribbon with some Latin words which he says, roughly translated, says, "Let us get the buggers before they get you."

Ever since he helped me with a matter concerning a dead model and I saved his animals from death at the city pound, we been friends and I called on him once or twice to get into places or stake places out because he's got this talent of disappearing into the walls through the most unlikely methods.

The guy in the bar and grill finally answers.

"This is Jimmy Flannery," I says. "Is Willy Dink around?"

"No," he says, "Willy ain't been around a day or two now."

"How's that?" I asks. "He ain't in trouble, is he?"

"Nothing like that, as far as I know. He said something about wanting to get some fresh air these warm nights. Maybe go over to Saganashkee Slough, where there's more trees and less homeless than Grant Park."

"What's he doing way the hell over there in the forest?" I says. "How's he going to get his calls?"

"He's got one of them phones you carry around with you."

"You happen to have a number?"

He gives me a number. While I'm dialing up, I'm wondering how Willy Dink's got a cellular phone when he can't pay the rent on a flat and lives in his truck. Of course there's always been the problem with landladies about the creatures he uses in his business, so even if he's fallen on good times and could afford a flat, he might not be able to find one anybody'd rent to him.

The phone rings way out there on the edge of the city and then Willy Dink picks it up.

"Is them birds I hear?" I says.

"Is that you, Jimmy?"

"What're you doing running around with a phone what costs forty dollars minimum a month to own."

"You should know better'n that, Jimmy," he says. "I made an arrangement."

"You found a way to pirate cellular phone service?"

"You know how to get into buildings, stores and offices, here and there, and you learn how to work these computers, you'd be surprised what you can do," Willy Dink says. "But I don't steal nothing from people," he quickly adds. "So what can I do you for?"

"I've got a little stakeout job for you," I says.

"Where?"

"Bridgeport?"

"Night or day?"

"A little of each."

"Inside or outside?"

"Your pick after you look the place over."

"Give me an address."

I give him the address.

"So you want to meet there and explain things to me?"

"Meet me at Schaller's Pump and we'll drive over together. That truck of yours is maybe too conspicuous."

"I ain't stupid, Flannery," he says, somewhat offended.

"I never said. Just meet me at the Pump."

I'm parked in front of the Eleventh Ward Democratic Headquarters across the street from Schaller's when a red Honda pulls up at the curb behind me.

I glance up at the rearview and see this short guy get out and start walking toward me. He's got something under his arm and something draped around his neck.

I twist around in my seat because I can't believe my eyes. I never seen Willy Dink dressed so sharp in gray slacks and a tweed sport jacket. He's even wearing a dark green hat with a feather in the band.

The package under his arm is the little dog, Timmy, and the bundle on his shoulder is his ferret, I forget its name.

I get out of the car thinking how you got to watch out or the whole world'll change on you while you got your back turned.

"What's going on here?" I asks. "Is this your Saturday-night-out outfit?"

"This is my professional look," he says. "I ain't going to look like a Gypsy no more, Jimmy. It's time I got into the new society."

"You crawl into walls dressed like that?"

"When I got a dirty job to do, I put on the pair of coveralls I got in the car. Is this a dirty job you got for me to do?"

"That depends on how and which end you're looking at," I says. "You want to drive over and case the stakeout with me or follow me in your fire engine?"

"I'll go with you and decide how to handle it," he says. "Then we'll come back here and you can buy me a beer before I go dry until the job's done."

He's talking like a professional or an agent from the Bureau of Investigation.

He gets in my car, tossing Timmy and the ferret in the backseat.

"You really got to get yourself a new set of wheels," he says.

So ten minutes later we're parked across the street from the three-flat that was once two three-flats.

"What am I looking for?" he asks.

"I want to see who goes in and out of that building in the next two or three days."

"Anything go on in there I should know about?" he asks.

"A woman was found dead, probably murdered," I says.

"The cops got the doors taped?"

"They're finished doing everything they intend to do," I says.

"We talking the rug and the broom here?"

"That's what," I says.

He's been looking around, up and down the street, up and down the buildings all around.

"I can't stake it out on the street," he says. "How's it set up inside?"

"I only know the top floor. I figure you can find out the rest for yourself."

"But it's only the third floor you're interested in?"

"I think so."

"So I won't stake it out from the lobby level either. I'll go inside. You want pictures?"

"They could be useful."

"Stills or tape?"

"Tape. I got to tell you, Willy, this new efficiency of yours is very impressive but it worries me a little bit."

"Don't you worry, it's the same old Willy Dink, Jimmy, but the world marches on and you got to change just to keep up. Okay, lets go get that beer. I don't want the neighbors should have too much time to start worrying what two men in a car are doing parked in a residential neighborhood."

I start the engine.

Willy's still looking at the conversion.

"A very handsome remodel," he says.

"You ought to see the inside," I says.

"Oh, I will," he says.

24

God is supposed to have rested on the seventh day, some people say Saturday, some people say Sunday, but I didn't rest.

All day Sunday I'm over to the house in Bridgeport working my tail off helping Mary, Charlotte, Sada and Janet Canarias decide which stuff of Delvin's and which stuff of ours is to be set aside for a garage sale. Which, I hope, could help make up some of the expenses of this move.

Some of the furniture, pictures and lamps is going to auction, also to make some money to pay for all this deferred maintenance and improvements.

I been given the job of sorting through photos, papers and documents, old newspaper and magazine clippings, making up my mind what I want to keep and what I'll donate to the Harold Washington Library if they want it.

There's other stuff what'll go to different charities.

So much stuff. A ton of stuff.

The women love the process. I hate the process.

"Driving you nuts, Jimmy?" Janet asks.

"I can't help feeling that I'm picking through things I shouldn't be picking through, putting my nose where it don't belong."

"It's got to be done," she says. "It's not only sorting through Delvin's possessions, is it?"

"I've got a problem."

"Talk about it?"

"I don't think so. Not yet," I says, waiting for her to make the offer a second time, which is only polite.

"Anything I can do to help?" she asks.

She looks at her watch. She's a busy lady. She's giving Mary a couple of extra hours here and she feels she really shouldn't waste a minute.

"It's help if you could tell me where I could find Mabel Halstead," I says, not getting into it the way I was intending to.

She looks at her watch again after just looking at it, the way busy people do.

"At the storefront," she says. "Every Sunday Mabel gives me half a day, sets up my appointment book for the week and checks my calendar for the month. Mabel's the best at that sort of organization I've ever seen. She even bought me a watch that can be programmed to sound a tiny alarm when an important appointment is coming up."

"A watch?"

"I leave it on my desk when I leave the storefront Saturdays and pick it up Sunday night or Monday morning."

"I don't know if I can keep up," I says.

"I know what you mean," she says.

"I don't know if I want to keep up," I says.

She leaves and a minute later Mary walks in and stands there watching me sort.

"There's so many boxes of letters and reports and old documents here," she says. "Are you making a dent?"

"I think maybe I should get us some help from the library," I says. "There's a lot of junk here but a lot of stuff that's historical, valuable even. Maybe we should get an expert in."

"Could you do that?" she says.

"I could do that. Just pile everything like that in here."

"There's three times as much again down in the basement," she says.

I must've groaned because she grins and says, "This is the first house move we ever really made, not counting me moving in with you," she says. "It'll be the last for a long, long time to come, if ever. So let's consider it an adventure. Are you hating it?"

"The books and papers is one thing. I'll help the librarian sort through it. There's even things I'll probably want to save for myself. But the rugs and chairs and dish towels and doilies, I don't know what to say when you ask me should we get rid of it, should we keep it."

"I don't want to shove you out of it, James. I don't want to leave you feeling that your opinion doesn't matter."

"The thing is," I says, "I got no real interest in whether you keep this chair, that table, or what. Except for Delvin's old leather chair and the rug what he used to throw over his knees. I'd like it if you could find a place for them."

"The chair needs upholstering," she says.

She don't have to tell me what I already know, but I understand why she did it. The next time I complain about the expense of something she thinks needs doing, she can bring it up to me that she didn't make any complaints when the chair I wanted to keep was done over.

I stand up from where I been squatting and try to get my knee joints back in place.

She comes up to me chest-to-chest and lays her cheek against mine.

"You are a man among men, James Barnabas Flannery." She kisses me and then backs away so she can watch my eyes and know what I say next is true. "You'd really rather not be in on the decisions?"

"Not these decisions," I says. "You make the house you'll be happy in and I'll be happy in it, too."

"Well, then, go on and have a day for yourself."

She kisses me again and then practically pushes me out the door so she can get with it. I'm not even down the steps when the four of them are laughing and carrying on and I realize I was throwing a wet blanket on their fun.

I go looking for Mabel Halstead, who used to be a man, used to be a cop and who has, even after the hormone shots and sex-change operations, a very deep voice.

I go down to the alderman's office which Janet Canarias lets me use.

I don't expect to see Mabel there. She was there practically every day and night while Janet was running for the seat on the council and worked part-time after she won it, but there wasn't enough in part-time work to keep her going and she went off to do other things, organizing a ring of prostitutes apparently being top priority. She still gives Janet an evening here and there but my hopes ain't high that she's going to be sitting in a chair waiting for me even if Janet expects her to be there on a Sunday. Except there she is.

She's reading a book and looks up when I come through the door.

"You look like a wreck," she says, and laughs.

It's the laugh I heard on the telephone.

"What took you so long, Jimmy?" she says, and now I recognize the voice I heard on the phone and on the speakerphone in the lobby of the double triplet over to Bridgeport.

She stands up and sticks out her hand, a masculine thing to do, and for a minute there, in spite of the head of curly hair and the eyeliner and the lipstick, I see Milton Halstead, the cop, looking out of this pretty face.

"I didn't recognize your voice until I just heard it coming out of your mouth," I says.

She almost blushes. "I was disguising it a little bit but

it's hard to really to that. Those electronic maskers do a good job but it's not the sort of thing I carry around with me. Are we going to sit down?"

That's a good idea because, like it or not, an average man stands next to a tall woman, it makes him a little bit nervous because it's outside the way things usually are.

"Why'd you call me and not the cops?" I asks.

"You want a coffee? A cup of tea? We've got some soft drinks in the fridge. Of course you know that. You use these offices, too."

"No, thanks," I says. "I'm all right. So why'd you even call anybody at all?"

"I wasn't going to. I was going to walk out and leave her there. That would've been the smart thing to do. Let the trick she was waiting for find her. Give him something to think about besides his unbecoming arrogance."

"You know who this client is?" I asks.

"Don't you?"

"I got a good idea but can we prove it?"

"I haven't got pictures but I've got his number in Fay Wray's little black book."

"Where'd you get it?"

"Lifted it out of her purse on my way out."

"Intending to use it for a little leverage?"

"Blackmail? That's not my game, Jimmy, but I don't blame you for the accusation."

"It wasn't an accusation. It was a question. Why'd you take it, then?"

"So nobody would lose it. In case corroborating evidence was ever needed."

"So does that mean you've got especially bad feelings against Lundatos?"

"I suppose my bad feelings about a man escalates in proportion to the money, fame, honor and power he's achieved. A school principal is guiltier than a teacher for patting a child on the ass, a United States representative has more to answer for if he's caught with his hand in the till than a city alderman."

"That's an interesting point of view," I says.

"You've got to pay back something if you've been luckier than others. The more you get, the more you owe. I'm not talking only money."

"But, I mean, besides this interesting speculation, do you have any particular, personal reason to dislike Lundatos?"

She shakes her head.

"So why was you there in the first place?" I asks.

"I had an appointment with Fay."

"You don't call her Mavis?"

"I call her by her working name because the meeting was about her work."

"You were trying to recruit her?"

"I don't recruit anyone, Flannery," Mabel says. "I'm not a fan of prostitution."

"Then I don't get it. You're in the business."

"It's more like I'm in the business of being a union organizer."

"Why did you arrange the meeting at Lundatos's apartment?"

"Convenience. Timing. I'm a busy woman and Fay Wray was a busy woman."

"All right, so the two of you decided to meet in the apartment of a man she was about to make love with."

"Service. Had serviced the night before."

"I beg your pardon."

"I just don't want any sugarcoating on it. Fay Wray was selling a service. I was trying to sell a service to her."

"Health insurance, annuities and life insurance?"

"That's correct."

"Are you a licensed broker?"

"I am."

"Is that how you make your profit?"

"Of course. I have to get paid for my time, don't I? You get paid for your time down in the sewers, don't you?"

"I don't go down in the sewers any more."

"I mean you might work for the party for nothing, just like I work for Janet Canarias for nothing, but everybody's got to have a job that pays the rent. Isn't that right?"

"Sure. I wasn't criticizing. I was only asking," I says. "You say you were also a kind of union organizer."

"You heard about COYOTE back in San Francisco?"

"Yes."

"Well, I thought the women of Chicago might have use for such a union. Only I'm calling it a guild."

"All right, then, back to the day Fay Wray got killed."

"I arrived at the building in Bridgeport at seven-thirty A.M. Right on the dot. I rang the bell from downstairs and a voice asked me who it was and I said my name."

"A man's voice or a woman's voice?"

"I don't know. Those lobby intercoms aren't exactly hi-fi. You know that. I thought a woman's voice, but I was expecting Fay Wray to answer. Now, thinking about it, I'm not so sure."

"Just like me on the telephone when you called me. I thought it was a man's voice. Then, later on, thinking about it, like you say, I consider how it might be a woman's."

Mabel grins. "Of course, we've got a rare situation here. I mean the hormones and surgery gave me tits, hormones and depilatories gets rid of the hair, but even though they cut off my major sex characteristic, I don't think anything did a hell of a lot of change my voice. I still sound like a foghorn."

"Very sexy," I says.

"Oh, do you think so?"

"I was merely making the observation that half of what you hear is what you see," I says.

"And I was merely accepting the compliment, Jimmy. I wasn't about to try and take it anywhere."

"So go on," I says, in a hurry to get off that road.

"I went on up."

"In the elevator?"

"No. It's one of the kind that only works with a key. I didn't mind walking up the stairs. The door was open at the top and I walked right in."

I'm living the minutes when I did the same thing.

"I walked into the big glass foyer, sunroom . . . whatever. Solarium. It took my breath, I can tell you. You'd never think a man like Lundatos would have the good taste."

"He probably didn't," I says. "His wife owns that building."

"I gave a yell," Mabel goes on. "Nobody answered, so I sat down, went through my briefcase and picked out some literature."

"I found some laying on the breakfast table."

"I figured that was part of the two and two you put together that got you here. I sat there for maybe two minutes. Then I gave another yell. Still no answer. I walked through the fuck pad. Nothing. I went back through the solarium into the gentleman bachelor's digs. Very British. All tweed and leather. I found her in the tub."

"Did you touch her?"

" Not on your life. I was a cop, remember?"

"You stick your finger in the bathwater to see how long she'd been in there?"

"Did you?"

"Yes," I says. "It was warm."

"It was hot when I tested it."

"Then you called me?"

"That's right."

"Why me?"

"Because you're about the only honest man I know, Jimmy. Scandal or no scandal back there in Washington, he's still got the power around Chicago. He's still got plenty of favors he can call in. If I'd called the cops, even the honest cops I used to know, they'd get boxed and conned into silence. So they found a dead whore. What's the big deal? Death by misadventure. Homicide by person or persons unknown."

"I don't know if I should thank you for your good opinion of me, but I owe you for the help you give me with them goons."

"I wasn't thinking about that when I called. I don't keep books, Jimmy."

"Let me ask you. Do you think Cleary knew about you trying to steal Fay Wray away from his stable?"

"Sure he did. Every pimp in town knows when somebody's trying to get their ladies under new management."

"They think you're just another pimp with a clever gimmick?"

"Sure they do. So would I, if I were in their shoes. Nobody does nothing for nothing, Jimmy. There's a payoff one way of another."

"And your payoff was just the commission on the premiums?"

"That's all. I wasn't even charging a fee for money management or acting as a CFA."

"CFA?"

"Certified financial adviser."

"Do you think Cleary would've come up here and bounced her around a little to teach her a lesson, and maybe it got out of hand?"

Mabel hesitates a long time before shrugging her shoulders.

"Do you think she scheduled a morning trick, as long as she had the use of the facility, and could he have arrived earlier than expected . . . before you got there . . . and they had a fight or the sex got rough?"

She give me another shrug.

"You really think it could've been Lundatos?"

Again she hesitates, then she says, "Think about this. You're an ex-congressman with some charges hanging over your head. Corruption charges mostly. Just a couple of whispers about moral changes which gets these conservative types all worked up. You're hoping to make it all go away by rallying the troops. Running for local office with an eye on the fifth floor in City Hall.

"Now think about this. You're a middle-aged prostitute with an invalid husband you're taking care of. It's never been in your bag of tricks to threaten a client with disclosure, but here's a once-in-a-lifetime chance for a big payday. One big payday that can get you out of the life. That can buy you and your crippled husband a little house up on a lake and a nest egg that, properly invested, can keep you both comfortable for the rest of your life."

"So you think she might have put the arm on him?"

"I think it's the most likely of the possibilities we've mentioned."

"You rule out accident?"

"I don't rule out accident. I've seen people who slipped in the tub, but not very often, and the victims were always much older than Fay Wray."

"So you think Lundatos might've done it?"

"He's the one looking to bury the investigation along with Fay Wray, isn't he? He's the one making you an offer he doesn't think you can refuse."

"How do you know that?"

"Hey, I was a cop, wasn't I? Once a cop always a cop, Jimmy."

25

Once upon a time, when I was walking the sewers all day and walking the precinct in the evenings knocking on doors for the Democratic Party, seeing what needed doing in the neighborhoods, a bachelor with nothing on my mind but washing my car on Saturday morning at the curb outside Joe and Pearl Pakula's grocery store downstairs from my flat on Polk Street, having supper every Wednesday night with my old man at Dan Blatna's Last Chance Saloon, until last night some politicians asked me to give up my virginity and hop in bed with them . . . I'm talking metaphors here . . . I lived a pretty simple life.

I been asked to give up my principles for a payoff before. I even lay down on top of the covers once or twice and had a little pillow talk about going along to get along, but I always kept one foot on the floor.

Then I met the lady what was to become my wife, and bought the building we still lived in to save it from the developers, and had a baby, and went to my father's and Mary's mother's wedding to each other, and got promoted until I was an inspector who didn't have to walk the pipes any more, except on rare occasions, and got promoted in the party, too, becoming the ward leader of the Twenty-seventh, which is a ward sinking into poverty and hardship no matter what I've tried to do to save it.

I'm going to night classes to learn how government is supposed to work and how to speak and write the English language better so I can hold my own in conversation with the important people who are treating me like one of themselves more and more.

And I seen the neighborhoods change, grow old and die, just like friends of mine, Mrs. Banjo and Chips Delvin and Father Mulrooney, has grown old and died. And many more to come, these old friends growing older. They look at me when we meet like they ain't sure they know me. Like they're trying to remember my face so they can take it with them on a journey they're about to take. Knowing their ticket's going to be punched pretty soon.

Old Dunleavy over to Streets and Sanitation. Carlucci and O'Ryan, cronies of my father's, what stop by to chew the fat, now and then. And Mike hisself. Going on a trip one of these days.

But not right now. Right now I'm being asked to break the promise I whispered to myself once upon a time, laying in bed, looking at the shadows made by passing cars on the ceiling of my bedroom.

I'm being asked to forget about the death of a woman I hardly knew, not because it would bring down the city government or close the bridges and tunnels, but because it would save a politician a little embarrassment. If, at best, what Lundatos swore was true, that he wasn't the person in the flat when Fay Wray died, and if, at worst, he was the one who killed her, on purpose or by accident, we're talking about an evil conspiracy no matter how you want to look at it.

We can just forget her, the cops, the State Attorney's Office, the Democratic Party. We can just sweep her under the rug or suck her up in the vacuum cleaner of our own self-interest, like she was a fur ball, and throw her in the garbage.

The crowd around that table in Dan Blatna's seem to know who the man is what called me in. That means they was contacted. That means somebody's trying blackmail. Even if Lundatos was nowhere near the building where Fay Wray was found dead, a man already under indictment for so many crimes and misdemeanors ain't going to be helped by a suspicion of consorting with prostitutes, let alone murder. That means, with these people who play a brand of ball I know about but ain't used to playing, this blackmailer could be in serious danger of being found floating in the river or sleeping the long sleep under the garbage out to the city dump.

"What are you thinking about?" Mary asks me at breakfast.

"Tennis," I says, because right that minute tennis pops into my head.

She's got this little grin on her face. I know she thinks it's funny sometimes how my head works.

"So what about tennis?"

"Sometimes I go out on the courts over to the school grounds and bat the ball around, you know?"

"You shouldn't," she says, being wife, mother and nurse. "You shouldn't play hard on Saturday afternoon when you've had no exercise all week."

"I don't play hard, you can count on that," I says. "But there's some of the players out there would like to be A players at some athletic club. They play three four-sets in a row, and then they talk about this Wimbledon champion, that World Open champion, like they can pick up some pointers to improve their own game."

"What's wrong with that?"

"Nothing wrong. But they're just dreaming because, no matter how good they are or think they are, the game they're playing, which they call tennis, ain't the same game these champions are playing."

"Which is by way of saying what, James?"

"That the game the people I had a couple of ginger ales with last night ain't playing the same game I'm playing."

"You'll work it out," she says.

I appreciate the confidence but it strikes me that things has changed. It used to be she would hunker right down and work my troubles out with me. Now she's getting to her feet and picking up Kathleen, who's getting to be a big girl and can do her own walking, but when Mary's in a hurry to start the day, she just sweeps up everything she wants or needs and carries them with her out the door.

"Hey," I says, which ain't much.

"We'll talk about it tonight," she says. "I've got to drop Kathleen off at day school, then do my shift at the free clinic, and then meet the house painters in Bridgeport. It's all right if I take the car?"

"Of course it's all right," I says. "But wait a second—"

"We really have to get a second car. It doesn't have to be new."

"What's this about the house painters? I thought we agreed that Mike and me and a few friends would paint the house."

"The interior. This is the exterior. It needs to be scraped and sanded and given two, maybe three, coats."

"Three coats?"

"It hasn't been painted in twenty years."

"Where's the money coming from?"

"We'll talk about that, too," she says.

"About what?"

"About me doing some private nursing, maybe," she says, and she's out the door before I get a chance to say another word.

I borrow Joe Pakula's pickup and go over to the conversion on Lowe. I want to talk to somebody who might know something about what goes on up there on the third floor, but every office is closed. There ain't a soul around and a few telephone calls to the different companies gets me nothing but them voices which instruct you to punch number one, punch number two, until they finally tell you to leave a message.

I got no reason to leave a message because I got a feeling everybody's been given an unexpected holiday until this unpleasantness blows over.

I got to talk to somebody. I think about Dunleavy, maybe the last old elephant left.

Dunleavy does his vaudeville trick on me. When I stop at the front counter and ask to see him, the clerk there sends me back and goes to the files.

Now that Streets and Sanitation is computerized, like practically every other department in the city, the file on me pops up even faster than when they had to tickle through a file drawer.

So by the time I walk back through the maze of corridors created by partitions set up for these office cubicles over the years, handwritten notes has landed on Dunleavy's desk.

It's a known fact that anybody actually caught using one of them computers is in danger of getting fired on the spot. That's the threat Dunleavy is supposed to've made in the heat of the irritation one day. So now every time he leaves his office to go out, he whistles to let them know he's coming.

The way old men do things to save themselves from their own ultimatums can be very complicated.

Anyway, Dunleavy's sitting there at his desk with the usual mountains of plat books, maps and papers piled everywhere.

"So, Jimmy Flannery, is it?" he says.

"It is, Mr. Dunleavy."

"Mike Flannery's boy."

"Yes, sir, Mr. Dunleavy. The very same," I says, repeating the ritual sentences like I been doing for years.

"That was a tasteful laying out you give old Delvin."

"And the funeral oration at the graveside?" I asks.

"Very tasteful," he says. "Also the funeral feast. Very tasty. What can I do you for?"

"There's a building over in Bridgeport. Two buildings, actually, what was made into one by these sort of enclosed breezeways."

"You got an address?"

I give him the numbers there on Lowe near Thirty-third.

"What would you like to know about them buildings?" he asks.

"Mostly who owns them."

He gives me a look. "And why would you like to know that? Now that you've a house in Bridgeport, just down the street from where the old mayor once lived, are you getting ideas about acquiring real estate?"

"I'm not looking to buy them buildings. Even if the thought ever entered my head, I ain't got the money."

"But soon could have it, ain't that right, Jimmy?"

"I beg your pardon," I says, which is the funniest damn thing to say when you expect somebody's ready to say something what could be insulting.

"I mean when you run for committeeman in the Eleventh . . . when you get it handed to you . . . you'll be rubbing shoulders with the power elite. Ain't that what they call it nowadays? The power elite?"

"I don't know what they call it or even who they might be," I says.

"Don't come all over dumb with me, Jimmy," the old man says.

"I wasn't saying I don't know who this power elite is, just that I don't spend much time rubbing shoulders with them."

He stares at me for a long time, peering at me like an old turtle with these lidded eyes with pouches under them, a man crowding the edges of life, going to be a hundred when the century turns.

"God Almighty, maybe you ain't as clever as they think you are. Maybe you really don't know that this invitation from Lundatos to run the Eleventh with him hand in hand is an invitation from the fifth floor."

"From the mayor?"

He nods.

"I hardly ever meet the man, let alone talk to him, let alone have any conversations about my political situation."

"You're being tapped on the shoulder. That's how it's done sometimes. Out of nowhere. Something happens that gets somebody high up's attention. They have their little talks. 'What about this Flannery? He looks a likely lad.' 'And so he is. A little headstrong. A little bit of a loose cannon. Apt to defy authority.' 'Wild and unsteady, is he?' 'I wouldn't say so. Not as wild as he used to be. Not lately, anyway. Got hisself a wife.' 'That's always good.' 'Got hisself a baby.' 'Even better.' 'Father was a fireman and a loyal precinct captain for many years.' 'God bless him.' You see, Jimmy, that's the way it goes."

He does all the voices and he's pretty good at it, this old actor what's seen it all and built hisself a structure of empire so complicated that it's a scramble, he don't want to know about, for everybody to get all he knows into them computers. To create some order. Otherwise, when he dies, the city will forget streets and alleys that only this old man remembers, and, who knows, like magic, parts of Chicago could just disappear.

"That building on Lowe is owned by Davidian and Associates, a holding company, which owns a majority interest in Parnell and Jones, a management company, which had a majority interest in Twenty-first Century Properties, a development company, which is fully owned by Carteret Enterprises, a leasing company, which is one of the major real assets of Higgens, Huggins and Burke, attorneys-at-law, one of the silent partners of which is Margaret Cooley Burke Lundatos. Which is, no doubt, what you already surmised."

"Oh, it figured, all right," I says, not telling him that I've already been told.

"Well, let me tell you, if you're also surmising other things. Leo would have had nothing to do with the death of that girl."

I'm about to correct him and say woman when I realize that any man under fifty is a boy and any woman under sixty a girl to a man Dunleavy's age.

"What can you tell me about Lundatos?"

"I got maybe twenty years on him. So I know about him, the way you know about him, from what I read. Maybe a little more."

"So you wouldn't know much about the kind of man he really is?"

"What you see is what you get," Mike says. "That was his trouble, wasn't it? He never tried to cover his tracks."

"Some people'd call that arrogance," I says.

"And some people'd call it being open and aboveboard."

"What would you call it?"

Dunleavy's thoughtful for a long time. I eat my lunch and let him work it through, how he wants to approach what he's got to say.

"He was a careful man at the beginning," Dunleavy says for starters. "You remember 1957?"

"How could I remember 1957? I wasn't even born."

"In 1957, Harvey Pullman, the state treasurer of Illinois, drops dead of a heart attack and they find half a million dollars in cash in his closet which sends the investigators along the money trail that leads to racetrack stock deals. Lundatos is on the Sanitary District Board at the time and in a position to do many favors for the track concerning water. Also sewage disposal. That's when he was first associated with Delvin. Some people, in fact, said that Delvin was his Chinaman."

"That's what Lundatos told me."

"Lundatos was among the beneficiaries of these racetrack deals. He first denies and then admits he's got shares .

. . I don't know how many, but substantial . . . in the Hanover Trotting Association."

"He could've bought them," I says.

"Probably did. A penny apiece. What I'm saying is that he knew how to dodge bullets even back then before he even made his run for the U.S. Congress. That happened the next year."

"With Mayor Daley's blessing is my understanding."

"Oh, yes, though Hizzoner couldn't understand why this young man what was doing so good in ward politics and had a future in Chicago would want to go back to D.C. so far from home," Dunleavy says. "The mayor was grooming him for his own job, you understand. But Leo's got different ideas and Richard J. goes along. Twenty years later, Lundatos is sitting there in the Congress and it comes out that he sponsored some legislation which helps some development projects of which this promoter, Eddie Ward, was trustee. There's a talk of conflict and so forth but Lundatos points out that the thousand bucks he put into one of the profitable ventures on which he made a hundred thousand had been put into a blind trust so how did he know what was going on?"

"And whoever raised the question believed that?"

"This Eddie Ward quit as trustee, Lundatos sells his interest, and it goes away."

"What you're saying here is Lundatos did what half the Congress does."

"Nothing special. Why not? Something's going to get done anyway and somebody asks you to grease the rails a little bit, what's to hurt? You're getting advice which you got no reason to think ain't advice from important and powerful people, so where's the danger? Where's the sin?"

Dunleavy rocks in his chair and makes a noise in his chest. At first I think he's choking on something and start to lean forward to slap him on the back, but he puts up his hand and says, "It's all right. It's all right. I'm just laughing."

"What're you laughing about?"

"I was just thinking. It ain't the big crimes that brings these people down, it's petty theft. They get in the habit of taking little favors. A free trip to the Bahamas. A free golfing week at Pebble Beach out there in California. A chauffeur-driven car you can park in front of a water hydrant without worrying you'll get a ticket."

"A lot of that?"

"As much as Lundatos wanted."

"Nothing out-and-out against the law, though?"

"Under the rules at the time. I'm not saying just according to custom. I'm saying under the sweet rules and regulations these congressmen make up for themselves, rules that let them convert stationery allowances they don't use into cash which they can put into their own pockets. And did to the tune of maybe five or ten thousand dollars each per year."

"I remember hearing something about that. Wasn't that privilege ended?"

"Around 1977."

"I just read the indictment against him in the *Weekly Congressional Record* down to the library," I says. "That was the year they claim he set up the means to milk his petty-cash account."

"So he wasn't being too careful any more."

"And he had a beard."

"What do you mean, a beard?"

"He had a couple of million dollars in unused campaign funds. He never needed it. He had a safe seat. The voters sent him back to Congress like they was just punching his train ticket."

"Until this last time."

"How was he to know things'd changed as much as they had? But at the time we're talking about, he had a couple of million the high rollers contributed to his campaign. Let him do what he wanted with the money. Under the rules, he could've tucked it under his arm and walked away with it."

"So why did he loot the petty cash?"

"*If* he looted it. Charged but not proven is the way it goes. Innocent until proven guilty. And for a while there, after his defeat, it looked like it's never come to a hearing let alone a criminal trial."

"Until a hooker's found dead in the bathtub in his high-rise hideaway," I says.

"Well, three floors don't make a high-rise, but I get your meaning," he says.

"So you ain't answered me. Why?"

He thinks a little bit.

"You take Nixon."

I make a face.

"Here's this fool what lets his aides talk him into snooping around Democratic Headquarters, see if they got any dirty tricks up their sleeve. He was paranoid they was out to steal the election away from him the way a lot of people thought they done when Kennedy defeated him. You remember?"

"Mayor Daley was supposed to have fixed the election results in Chicago, which won the state, which gave Kennedy the electoral votes he needed to win," I says.

"That's the way they played that tune," Dunleavy agrees. "So these fools go out and hire a bunch of gazooneys couldn't rob a kiddy's piggy bank."

"The plumbers."

"They was plumbers all right. Okay, it hits the fan, a little second-story job that went astray. Forget about it. Dummy up. But this mental giant's got everything down on tape, including the fuck this and fuck that. That kind of language we know everybody uses every day but we're not ready to admit. Especially not if you intend to have some woman transcribe the notes into hard copy."

He's using a computer phrase, hard copy, so he gives hisself away. He ain't all that dumb about the new-age technology that's taking over the world.

"Maybe all these schmucks think the way that recent

bad-boy senator thinks," he goes on. "Maybe he can get his secretaries worked up with the dirty language. Anyway, when it all comes out, why don't Nixon just dump the tapes, which, as a point of historical fact, was recorded on the system put in by Kennedy. Anybody asks, he tells them to go to hell. He burnt them. They was his tapes and he burnt them."

"But he was arrogant," I says.

"In the true meaning of the word. To make a claim without the right. Nixon thought he could fight the battle on the grounds of executive privilege, which would have been a very useful principle for him to be able to claim in future."

"And what principle was Lundatos trying to establish?"

"Laissez-faire. One. An economic doctrine that's against government regulation of commerce. Two. Noninterference in the affairs of others. He was dumb for doing it the way he did it, but I really think he was fighting for the system of perks and privileges the Congress has enjoyed for many years. His mistake was in thinking the rest of the club would back him up given the temper of the times."

I sit there chewing it over.

"Is there anything else I can do for you, Jimmy?"

"You can tell me how come a commercial enterprise can do business in a residential neighborhood."

"There's an exception for professional undertakings. Doctors, dentists, accountants, lawyers and so forth."

"There's always exceptions, ain't there?" I says, getting to my feet.

"Well, you should know, Jimmy. You're managing to find them all the time."

26

I go see Abe Binderman over at the Crime Lab. We've been friends from a long ways back when I convinced this man what had a nose like a forty-nine-cent pickle that looks wasn't everything to women. A good heart and other physical considerations could loom large in their consideration. He's been married for a long time now, with I don't know how many kids.

Even so he don't greet me with all that much enthusiasm, having learned that when I come see him at his place of work, I've usually got a favor to ask, which I always make plain he don't have to honor in spite of the good turn I done him.

"I'm afraid to ask to what do I owe the honor of a visit," he says, "because you might tell me."

"You get the medical examiner's report on one Mavis Hovannis?"

"Complete with vaginal, anal and oral swabs, stomach contents and fingernail scrapings," he says.

"So tell me," I says.

"There's nothing to tell. They were sent and then they

were followed by a request for their return. Is this another alleged crime you're going to make a mess about?"

"You know, Abe, maybe you been too long in this job. When you start thinking that it's better to keep your nose and your desk clean, your eyes and your mouth shut, then you could be in danger of not doing the job the people pay you to do."

"You can't make a case of corruption or malfeasance for every body that turns up in the city of Chicago," he says.

"Mavis Hovannis, aka Fay Wray, is the only body we're talking about here. You have a chance to look at the specimens they sent you?"

He hesitates a tick too long and I know that he did more than just take a look.

"You got curious, didn't you, Abe? They ask for the return of this evidence and it makes you curious."

"I looked over the report very carefully and made some serology tests."

"How about DNA?"

"Are you crazy? Those tests don't cost a nickel or a dime. They aren't routine. They're only done on special request."

I take the handkerchief Lundatos had bled on out of the envelope in which I put it to carry around.

"What's this?" Abe says.

"It's a bloodstained handkerchief," I says. "You need a special order to test it for me?"

"Is that all you want me to do? I can do that."

"I want you to also tell me if it matches the blood type found in the sperm Hackman took from the body cavities of Fay Wray."

"All I can do is tell you if there's a gross comparison," he says.

"That's enough."

"It won't do you much good. I sent the samples back as requested."

"I want to thank you, Abe," I says.

"Well, I don't forget the favors you've done for me. Also . . ."

"Also what?" I says, when he don't finish the thought.

"Also I don't always just clear my desk and keep my nose clean. This woman struggled. There was skin under the nails. I'll see if there's a match with your bloodstains in case there's nothing in the sperm. Everybody's not a secretor."

I don't ask for the technical explanation of that, but just stand there listening, glad of the fact that he's leveling with me.

"There was froth in her lungs," he goes on.

"Nobody's trying to say she wasn't drowned," I says.

"But I've got an idea they're not entertaining the notion that she was held down. There's severe pressure bruising on the chest."

I thank him again. He stops me at the door.

"One thing, Flannery," he says. "I'm pleased to help you, but I see no reason to cut my own throat. When I give you the results of the tests on that handkerchief, I want you to forget where you got them."

"I know the rules, Abe."

27

It's in the papers, the *Sun-Times* and the *Tribune*. Joe Medill of the *Trib* and Jackie Boyle of the *Sun-Times* both devote their columns to the possibilities of a local scandal involving a dead prostitute and a disgraced national politician.

Anybody who knows anything about the way decent newspapers work knows that they go running around checking their facts, digging in here and there. Turning over rocks. Greasing palms and filling pockets if they have to, what with the competition nowadays. Looking for Deep Throat.

Ever since Watergate everybody what's got a column or access to a paper, even a shopping rag, thinks they could be Woodward and Bernstein.

They're also very careful to check their facts because of what my political science teacher calls "this most litigious of all nations."

So I'm not surprised when Jackie Boyle finds me over to the Homewood Tavern having a root beer out of the wood, which is a very rare drink to find in this day and age.

"Can I buy you another?" Boyle asks.

"One's my limit," I says, "but if you're having a beer, I'll buy you one. Anything stronger or more expensive you'll have to do on your own."

"Won't be that way forever," Boyle says, making like he's grabbing the handle of a stein to indicate to the bartender that he'll have a draft.

"You'll have to run that train by me one more time," I says.

"It won't be long before you'll have a slush fund which will enable you to buy a friend a drink of his or her choice anytime and anywhere."

"I still ain't aboard," I says.

"The word on the street is that you've been invited to sit at the table with the movers and shakers."

"Oh?"

"The word's also on the street that you've been offered a seat on the train what's running on the fast track. Lundatos, they say, wants you to share in his rehabilitation. Now that he's home from the wars inside the Beltway, he's going to try and pick up where he left off thirty years ago. You've been made a confidant, a colleague, the keeper of secrets."

So what he's saying is that the offer to run for committeeman when Lundatos runs for alderman in the Eleventh comes after the facts concerning Fay Wray and her unhappy demise. In matters like this, reporters play fast and loose with timing, putting the cart before the horse if it makes a better dirtier story.

"I don't know what to say to that," I says. "Would it do any good to deny knowing what you're talking about?"

"You know I'll always listen to what you got to say, Jimmy," he says like a cat sitting down to make a meal of a mouse.

"I read your column," I says. "Who's your source?"

He sticks his finger alongside his nose, claiming professional confidentiality.

"You give me a laugh, Jackie," I says. "You expect me

to give you names, dates and places, and you give me the sanctity of the newsman's confessional back. Is that all you can do for me? Where's the favor for favor? The old quid pro quo?"

"You notice, in the column, I only give you a passing glance? I don't tie you in tight with the possibility of a conspiracy to compound a felony here?"

"To what?"

"To cover up a goddamn murder."

"You just dived off the high board, Jackie. What makes you think the death of that lady was murder?"

He gives me his best lopsided grin.

"Ah, Christ, Jimmy, don't I know the moon is made of green cheese and all and all?"

When Boyle gets cute and Irish on you, you can bet he's losing patience and if you don't watch out you'll find yourself glowing like a neon sign in a blind item in his column.

"But you don't know and I don't know," I says, trying to be as earnest about it as I can. "Nobody knows. It's still under investigation."

"You telling me they're not going to just close and seal the file and forget about it?"

"I'm telling you I ain't forgetting it."

"You ain't the cops."

"That's what I'm saying, Jackie. I ain't the cops and I ain't said yes to running for anything with anybody and I'm telling you I still got it under investigation."

He looks at me for a long minute.

"You know what, Flannery?" he says. "It's a funny thing but over the years I come to have more faith in you than the cops or practically any-goddamn-body else."

"So what you're saying is you'll take my word and keep this story from moving to the front page if I keep you informed of what I find out?"

"There's your favor for favor. Your tit for tat."

"Quid pro quo," I says, correcting him. "You going to quote me, quote me right."

"You sure you won't have another root beer?" he asks.

I have practically this same conversation with Joe Medill, the columnist for the *Tribune* over to the Goat.

It's while I'm there, still having a conversation with him, making the same promises of giving him the exclusive when I know it, because making promises to columnists is like making promises to thieves, that Fred Hennesy, the white-haired driver Lundatos brought back with him from Washington, taps me on the shoulder and asks me if he can have a word.

Medill's about to leave anyway, having squeezed me for everything he could get, which is a lot less than what he'd hoped he'd get, so I say good-bye to Medill and invite Hennesy to take his stool.

"We ain't staying," Hennesy says.

"We?"

"You and me and my helper outside."

"Helper to do what?" I asks.

"To see that you don't trip and hurt yourself getting into the car."

It ain't exactly a threat but neither is it what I'd call a polite invitation. I decide not to make a thing about it, though I'm tempted to step on his shoeshine. Wherever he wants to take me, I decide it might be worth my time to go.

The Diet Coke I just drank on top of the root beer is making me feel bloated. A belch rises up and comes out of my mouth like a cannon shot.

"Well, that's better than a fart," Hennesy says.

We walk out to the limo waiting at the curb in a No Parking zone. There's a cop with the checkerboard cap band standing right there with his back to us. I wonder does he have a twenty in his pocket he didn't have before or is a nod all it takes.

"You get in the back," Hennesy says, holding the door open for me.

He gets in the front.

"This is my nephew, Billy Hennesy, my brother's grand-son," he says.

Billy turns around and gives me a big grin. He's the kind of kid you like right off the bat but I see these big Irish kids with the faces of angels and the soft voices of saints break a man's jaw, so I reach out and shake his hand just to let him know we're all friends there in the car.

He drives us over to Delaware, a couple of blocks from the Water Tower, to Cricket's, this restaurant in the Tremont Hotel.

When we pull up at the curb, Fred jumps out and opens the door for me again. I'm beginning to see what's to like about all this service somebody like Lundatos has gotten used to these last fifteen, twenty years.

"You coming?" I asks.

"Not my place," he says. "Go ahead on in. She's waiting for you."

I walk into the lobby and then into the restaurant off to the side.

It's a place I been in once or twice, but only once or twice, the prices being a little rich for my blood.

There's toys on shelves and counters all over the place. It's like the theme of the place. Toys. Important women gather here on a weekly basis, deciding on the cultural life of the city.

I can see Maggie Lundatos's silver hair practically glow-ing in the cool shadows at the back of the room. She's looking at me and smiling softly.

I walk back feeling like I just grew six inches, that I'm an attractive man of some importance.

"Sit down, James," she says, and I wonder what sixth sense she's got that tells her calling me James, something only my mother . . . God rest her soul . . . and my wife ever did on a regular basis, is going to touch my heart. "I'm about to order a shrimp salad. Does that sound good to you? Or perhaps you'd rather a small steak."

"I just had a hamburger and fries over to the Goat," I says.

"I've heard of that place. Was the hamburger any good?"

"Well, it's the place where all the press reporters hang out."

"You know how to answer a question without being disloyal," she says. "Something to drink, then?"

"A Diet Coke if they got it."

"Oh, I'm sure they've got it."

She glances up in back of me and I know there's a waiter there taking the order.

"I asked you to meet me alone because I want to make a personal appeal to you on behalf of my husband."

All of a sudden the chair I'm sitting in doesn't feel comfortable and I wiggle around a little trying to settle in.

She reaches out a hand and touches my sleeve.

"I'm not trying to embarrass you or put you on the carpet, James," she says.

I feel the color rising up out of the collar of my shirt. It upsets me a little that she's sitting there reading me like a book.

"Oh dear, there, I've gone ahead and done it again," she says.

"I ain't used to a woman like yourself treating me like I was somebody so important that she makes a special plea for my help."

"Important, yes, but useful might be the better word," she says. "You're a rare fellow, Flannery. A man with a reputation for absolute honesty in things that matter. Compassionate yet pragmatic. As tough and tenacious as a junkyard dog."

My mouth must've twitched.

"You're aware that's what many people call you?"

"Oh, yes. It's got me in some trouble."

"Trouble with the first team?"

"Plenty. The last time I tangled with them I ended up walking the pipes for a while."

"Did you ever stop to wonder why, if you're so much trouble, so disobedient, so independent, that they haven't just kicked you out? Fired you from your job and kicked you out of the party."

The waiter comes with my Coke and her salad. I take a sip, waiting for her to go on.

"Because they've had an eye on you for a very long time. You've been the subject of dinner conversation, in houses into which you've never even stepped a foot, for years. Your shenanigans have given a lot of powerful people a lot of laughs and that's never a bad thing as long as the laughter isn't derisive. If you'd been a lapdog, licking the hand that spanked you from time to time, or an attack dog who went biting and slashing every time it was punished, you'd be just another ward heeler standing by to do the little tasks and dirty chores required to keep the city running. You might have risen as high as someone like O'Meara, who's a very successful man according to his lights. You'd be welcome to sit among the alpha dogs but you'd never have a shot of being one yourself."

I know chicken fat and I know honey cake and I been buttered and sweetened by the best, but Maggie Lundatos is the best I ever seen. She's flattering the hell out of me because she wants a big favor for Leo and for herself and she's making it sound like it's not about them but all about me. My ambitions. My career. My chances to . . .

My head don't want to take it any further because I feel the sharp edge of ambition slicing at me and I get a hint of what they mean about somebody having fire in the belly.

"You've shown them just the proper streak of independence," she goes on. "By accident or design I'm not yet quite sure but, at the moment, I'd put my money on your sincerity. You can go all the way, as far as you want to go, James Flannery. It's up to you."

Some people think I'm sort of innocent when it comes to women but I ain't all that innocent. I've had my share of experiences before I married my wife and some offers since, which I never accepted. I know how women say one thing but mean another, especially when they're offering favors of a sexual type but don't want to risk rejection. Women are the best at letting the other party reach for the candy and then letting them have it or pulling it back, claiming misunderstanding, if the invitation ain't accepted in exactly the right way.

She keeps on reading me with them blue eyes and I can see she ain't no patrician born with a silver spoon in her mouth but an Irish girl from the Thirty-eighth Ward, the third daughter of eight children, four girls and four boys, her father a steelworker before they closed them down and a drunk thereafter. Headstrong and willful, she met and fell in love with a Greek, not as bad as maybe a Jew or an Italian, but bad enough in the Irish Catholic family she come from.

She was right there with Leo every step of the way and there was many who said she was the one who urged him to aspire to national offices, maybe the presidency, when he was all set to walk the road to the mayor's office on the fifth floor of City Hall. There was some that claimed she slept Leo's way to the position of power he finally achieved, but I don't believe that she ever did. But these was all whispers. There wasn't a soul that would swear to anything or could say more than that they heard about this or that from a friend of a friend of a friend.

"I'm not being coy," I says, playing my own little game of double meaning. "I ain't waiting to be begged or bought. I've always had a lot of trouble with things being covered up even if they're being covered up for very good reasons. On the other hand I guess it's true when people say I'll take the other side in an argument just to be a pain in the neck. Which ain't exactly true, but I understand what they mean. I'm tempted to take Congressman Lundatos—"

"Leo, for Christ's sake," she says, getting a little impatient with me. "We're asking you to jump into bed with us. You've got the right to call him by his first name."

I caught the little slip but I don't think it was a little slip. Going to bed with Lundatos and going to bed with her is two different issues here.

"Not if I find myself in a situation where I might have to do him harm," I says.

She pushes aside her salad. She's only had three or four bites, but she pushes it aside and glances up over my shoulder again, which is enough to have a waiter there to take her plate away. She orders a double espresso in a voice under perfect control.

"In what way could you or would you do Leo any harm?"

"I was dragged into this situation by a lady by the name of Mabel Halstead."

"I know all about the lady who was once a man."

"I found the woman who called herself Fay Wray dead in the bathtub."

"I know all about her, too."

I don't ask the question. I just look at her.

"Fay Wray and others," she says. "I know Leo's had his playmates here in Chicago whenever he's come back to check with his constituents. But that's between my husband and me, wouldn't you say?"

"I'd say it maybe could be between you and your husband and Fay Wray. She deserves a little consideration, a little common decency, and maybe a little justice."

I'm sitting there wondering where the hell that all come from. I ain't used to delivering sermons.

Maggie Lundatos looks at me like she's a little surprised, too, and then she says, "Don't you worry, James, everybody'll get what they deserve before the dust settles on this one."

28

Mavis Hovannis is having a service followed by cremation over to Saint George Church on Ewing and Ninety-sixth, on the Southeast Side, Tenth Ward, Fast Eddie Vrdolyak's old stamping ground.

When I get there about ten o'clock in the morning, in time for a ten-thirty service, there's hardly anybody there. Just a couple of the old neighborhood women you can expect to find in Catholic churches practically any hour of the day or night until closing time.

And Mabel Halstead's sitting all the way down front, staring at the open coffin, which is up there in front of the altar on a draped catafalque.

I genuflect and make the sign of the cross at the top of the aisle, more out of respect than conviction, and go down to kneel on the prayer bench.

Mavis Hovannis . . . Fay Wray . . . her red hair blazing against the cream-colored satin, her mouth red with lipstick, lays there like she's sleeping.

I never seen it to fail at a viewing how somebody, in fact more than one person, goes on about how good the corpse looks. Like they're sleeping. Mostly they look dead to me but if anyone was to say that the lady in the coffin looked like she was sleeping, I'd say it was very true.

I don't actually pray the way some people say you're supposed to pray, but I say a few words in memory of the lady I met only the once but probably won't ever forget.

I get off my knees and turn my back on her, walking over to Mabel Halstead's pew and sliding in beside her.

"Hello, Jimmy," she says. "Not much of a turnout, is it?"

"It's only five after," I says.

"You can keep one hand in your pocket. You'll only need five fingers to count the mourners."

Well, Fay Wray does better'n that but not much better.

Around ten twenty-five there's maybe seven people, not counting the two old regulars, sitting scattered throughout the church, hardly anybody sitting with anybody else, a handful of loners.

I excuse myself and go up the aisle and out of the church to see if there's many more just arriving, just in time to see a hired limousine, equipped with one of them side lifts for wheelchair entry, pull up at the curb.

The uniformed driver gets out from behind the wheel and another man with a black mourning band on his sleeve gets out on the passenger side. The two of them take Hovannis's folding wheelchair out of the trunk and then help Hovannis, still locked into that terrible cage of steel and leather, struggle into it.

He looks up at me and don't exactly nod but sort of compresses his chin into the leather chin cup, like he's thanking me for coming.

The two men, the driver and the other man, what looks like he could be Hovannis's brother or cousin, lift Hovannis and the chair and carry it up the steps and into the church.

I got inside.

Mabel's gone.

*   *   *

The ceremony's short and sweet, the priest saying the usual nice things about the departed, no mention of her flawed humanity, her struggle to keep going, her courage about taking in a man who done her wrong and caring for him and loving him in spite of everything.

At the end the priest makes the announcement that sepulture will take place in the columbarium over to the Bohemian National Cemetery on North Pulaski Road. That's way up in Albany Park across the river from Greektown and it's where Mayor Anton Cermak, who got shot dead when an assassin tried to kill FDR, is buried.

I watch them get Hovannis back in the limousine. I follow them in my own car. There's maybe two or three cars going up there but it's hard to tell because we don't stay in line like we were a funeral cortege. We don't follow a hearse or a flower car because there ain't any.

I got a feeling, the efficient way things is being done more and more nowadays, that the remains of Fay Wray will be waiting for us up there in a bronze jar, ready to be cemented into a wall.

Which they are.

Mabel's waiting for the funeral party up there, but she don't come over to stand with the rest of us and disappears again before the last prayer is said.

29

Fay Wray's in a jar in a wall. It would be easy to let her rest there and forget about how she died.

I got a new house to move into. Things to sell. Things to give away. Things to throw out.

I got a lot to think about. Do I want to move my political interests out of the Twenty-seventh into the Eleventh? Do I want to take Lundatos up on his offer and forget all about his possible involvement with Fay Wray?

What can I prove? Nothing? What can I even find out that will convince me or anybody else that Lundatos could've been the man what had sex with her one night and killed her the next morning?

It looks like blackmail could've been a motive. Fay Wray could've decided that, with all the ex-congressman stole from the public purse, she was entitled to a little of it to make up for all the hard luck in her life.

Just about everybody's in on keeping the whole thing quiet. Even Medill and Boyle ain't following it up in their columns. They got no place to go with it.

Mabel Halstead, the one who knew enough to blow the

whistle when she found Fay Wray in the bathtub and then
dragged me into it because she was afraid it would get
covered up, ain't saying anything about it any more.
Didn't say anything at the church. Didn't try to urge me
to keep on trying to do something at the cemetery.
Ducked me instead. Disappeared and ain't called me
since.

Because, maybe, like Shanker said, they had the matter
taken care of.

I don't feel very well. I feel like I'm coming down with a
cold and, like everybody knows, a summer cold can be a
bitch. I'm thinking maybe I'll crawl into bed and toss the
covers over my head. Nip the cold in the bud. Put my troubles to sleep for a couple of days.

I get a call from Willy Dink.

"I got something to show you," he says.

I'm on the edge of the telling him to forget the whole
thing but, instead, I tell him to come on over to the flat on
Polk Street where we still got our television set and VCR.

I got very little to offer him but he don't want anything
anyhow.

The only thing in the room is two kitchen chairs, a folding table and the portable television what we used to keep
in the bedroom, plus the VCR so I can watch a movie by
myself if I want, what with Mary setting up the house over
in Bridgeport, rearranging the last of the furniture which
she had took over the day before. It was like I got moved
out of my flat piece by piece so that by the time I really noticed, it was all over and done. Except for moving the furniture around, like I say, during which Mary said I only got in
the way.

"So what have you got to show me?" I asks.

Willy Dink puts the cassette into the player and punches
the start button.

"Nothing much," he says. "Which is why I'm here to

show you what little I got and advise you to drop the surveillance."

He's very crisp and businesslike. I don't know how much I like this new Willy Dink.

The camera's shooting down into the lobby of the conversion, pointing toward the elevator. He's cut the tape so I don't have to sit through hours of nothing.

Then I see a man walk across the floor of the lobby right to the elevator. He's got white hair like a lion's mane. I don't even need to see the face to know that it's Lundatos. He puts a key into the lock in the elevator door and gets into the cage. It runs up out of sight.

"Were you in the wall?" I asks.

"I had the camera fixed in the space between the ceiling and the floor above. I had it rigged to turn itself on when the front door was opened. It didn't get many people. Everybody in that building seems to be on vacation. There was a couple of messengers dropping envelopes in the slots but they never went above the second. The elevator's only for the top floor."

"I know," I says.

I'm watching the tape, thinking that Lundatos, what claimed he didn't even know his wife owned such a building or even where it might be located, has a key to the place and here he is making a beeline for the elevator and putting the key in the lock like he's done it a lot of times before.

"So there's that," Willy says as the tape briefly goes to snow. "I couldn't plant cameras in every room. I ain't got that kind of equipment yet. So I picked the bedroom next to the bathroom where the victim was found. Also the sunroom with the wall of glass and the living room in the adjoining flat. I covered what I could."

Now I'm watching Lundatos walking around the big sunroom like a man what knows his way around, touching this and that, looking for something or maybe making sure there's nothing.

He disappears out of camera range and reappears in the

bedroom. He touches a lot of things again and then takes a
small duffel bag out of an otherwise empty closet. He puts
the robe and slippers, and a set of pajamas taken from the
end table drawer, into it.

"So that's all of it," Willy Dink says as the tape goes to
snow again.

"When I think about all the things I missed on this one, I
could cry," I says.

"Don't beat yourself up. You ain't a cop."

It didn't help.

I make an appointment to meet with Lundatos over to the
Donovan Playground Park on Sangamon. I ask him to meet
with me alone.

He's waiting for me on a bench under a tree. Fred Hennesy's standing by this black sedan parked at the curb some
distance away.

It's suppertime and very quiet in the park or maybe it's
only that my head feels like it's filled with cotton.

Lundatos don't get up but reaches up to shake my hand.

"You came to say no to my offer," he says.

"Yes, sir, I did."

"You mind telling me why?"

"Maybe I just don't have the ambition," I says. "No fire
in the belly."

He nods like he understands that there's a lot of different
kinds of ambition.

"Things was simple when I started out in politics," I
says. "All I seen was a chance to chew the fat with people,
which is something I like to do, and maybe do favors for
my neighbors, people what can't help themselves. I know
some people'd say that's because I want to feel important,
better or smarter than everybody else. Maybe there's something to that. I don't know. All I can do is live inside my
skin. Live my own life. I don't compare myself with anybody else. I figure that's a waste of time. And I sure don't
want to be anybody else because that's just damned fool-

ishness. My old Chinaman always said to me, don't complain and don't explain. That's the way I want to live my life, with as few things to feel sorry for as I can manage and as few things to have to make excuses for as is practical."

"Don't we all," he says. "So are you telling me that associating with me would be a danger to your good feelings about yourself?"

"I guess that's one way of putting it," I says, "except I ain't making a judgment about you one way or another. The judgment I'm making is about me."

"You've been pretty square with me up to now, Flannery. Don't spoil it by stroking me just to shrug me off. You think I'm guilty as charged, don't you?"

"You mean about these federal indictments? I suspect you dipped into the petty cash and the stamp fund and maybe cut some corners with the congressional stationery store. I don't doubt that you used a government car and driver for your personal use and accepted vacations and weekend junkets here and there. But that's just taking a free newspaper or a cup of coffee when you're a beat cup. I don't think it corrupts the system. If it was only that, I might run with you in the Eleventh and stand up for you even if I decided not to run."

"Then it's the business about the call girl," he says.

"I got tape on you walking into that building and using a key to go up to the top floor on the elevator."

He's about to give me a lie about how he got the key from his wife because, out of curiosity, he wanted to see the place, but something in my expression stops him. He waves his hand, telling me to go on, like he knows there's more.

"I saw you going through the flat, picking up the robe and slippers you left there. Packing them into a duffel with the pair of pajamas you wore the night before Fay Wray died."

He don't say nothing. He turns his head. A breeze kicks up and ruffles his hair, blowing it around like it was milkweed. He ain't a lion with a heavy mane but an old man with thinning hair whirling around his head.

"If my wife can forgive me my transgressions, why can't you?" he says.

"Because I never loved you when you was young. Because I got no good times together to remember."

"Maggie had red hair when we were young," he says, like this is supposed to make me understand his desire for a redheaded prostitute and forgive him for betraying his wife for a memory of her.

"What comes next?" he says.

"You mean what am I going to do about Fay Wray?"

He gives a little nod, waiting for the verdict.

"I think you should retire," I says. "These federal indictments are probably going to go away. You done a lot of good things while you was in public life. Let the record stand."

"You're telling me not to run for alderman or you'll show those tapes? Make a case against me? Hold me up to public scrutiny here in my hometown?"

"I wouldn't insult you with threats," I says. "I'm just saying that I know I hit the wall on this. If you caused Fay Wray's death, I got no way to prove it. I'm ready to leave it at that and live with the fact that you can't always pick justice up like it was a lucky penny."

I leave him there, his face turned to the evening breeze again. White hair a cloud around his head.

30

I go over to see Abe Binderman. He's got the test results for me. The serology shows that the blood on the handkerchief comes from the same person what left the semen. He hands me the data.

"I don't know what you're going to do with this. I expect, if this is a sensitive matter involving important people, you might have trouble finding the original reports."

"But I know you keep copies on your computer," I says.

"That's confidential material. You'd need authorization."

"You also take a diskette home with you," I says.

"I'd have to deny it," he says. "This is getting too complicated and dangerous."

I hand him back the reports on the blood, which I could probably prove belonged to Lundatos and matched the semen samples, if I could get them into a court of law.

"Tear it up, Abe. I got no use for it."

Abe frowns and stares at me.

"What's this, Flannery? You ready to be part of a cover-up?"

"I don't see the profit in it," I says, and leave, letting him think what he wants to think about that.

I got to tell you the truth. Though I did my bit over the new house, I didn't really pay much attention to what was really being done by Mary and all her relatives and friends.

The night I put the two kitchen chairs, the folding table, the portable television and the VCR into my car and locked the door to the empty flat for what was really the last time, nobody's around the building. Even Joe and Pearl Pakula's store closed.

It's like walking out of a life that has nothing or nobody in it.

I knew I'd be going back, now and then, to do this and that, but this is really good-bye and there's nobody there to say it back to me.

I go up on the roof and lean on the rail. I look out across the city and these streets where I lived almost half my life. It's all around me, down there, the neighborhood.

I go back downstairs and lock the door, which really don't need locking, empty as it is, and walk down the six flights of stairs to the street.

I drive off, not knowing exactly what's waiting for me in Bridgeport.

What's waiting for me is a housewarming party.

The outside of the house has still got the scaffolding up. There's still plenty to sort out in the attic and down in the basement. A couple of rooms still need repainting and there's floors that need resanding, but mostly it's done.

I walk into a hall that smells like lemon oil and spices. The spices is coming from the kitchen, where I know somebody's cooking a turkey and maybe a ham.

Everybody shouts, "Welcome home!" when I walk into the parlor.

It looks like all the neighbors from the building on Polk, including Joe and Pearl, is there, plus Janet Canarias and

Mabel Halstead, my old man and my mother-in-law, Aunt Sada and the Chapmans and . . . well I could go on naming them . . . just about everybody who brings joy to my life.

Even old Dunleavy, who gets up out of this chair what smells of new leather and insists that I take it.

"Sit in this chair what was your old Chinaman's chair," he says. "Go on. Go on. I'll just sit on one of them wooden kitchen chairs you brung," he says, doing me a favor and making me feel guilty both at the same time. The spirit of Delvin ain't far away.

I sit down and somebody hands me a glass of ginger ale and somebody says the food's ready and somebody else tells me to stay where I am and they'll get me a plate.

So everything's hunky-dory, except that the memory of Fay Wray and what I ain't doing about it still haunts me.

And even though I made up my mind about not running for committeeman in the Eleventh, wanting nothing to do with Lundatos and that crowd, I know I still got a lot of explaining to do to all the people who had hopes and ambitions for me. I still ain't figured out how to deal with the dreams people you love want you to pursue.

A deep voice says to me, "Penny for your thoughts, Jimmy?"

I come out of my fog to see Mabel Halstead looking at me with this sad expression on her face. She's so tall she has to hunker down to get at eye level with me.

"They ain't worth a penny, Mabel."

"You know, I've always appreciated it," she says.

"What's that?"

"You never asked me to explain what I did."

"Well, you never complained to me about it, so I figured it was none of my business."

"Don't complain and don't explain," she says.

"Which ain't to say I ain't willing to listen anytime you feel you want somebody to talk to," I says.

"Well, I want somebody to talk to right now," she says.

We both look around the room, crowded with people, so

noisy with a dozen conversations that we're actually shouting a little so we can hear one another.

"Let's got into what Mary likes to call my study," I says.

"Does it have a television and a tape deck?"

"I think we got three or four of each around the place," I says. "Delvin's, Mrs. Thimble's and the ones we had in our living room. I even got one of each from the bedroom, out in the car."

Mabel grabs my hand and helps me up out of the chair. It's like she's lifting a feather, the strength she's got. We walk down the hall to the back.

There's still work to be done in this room but it's got Delvin's old rolltop desk in it and the wooden swivel desk chair, plus a small couch and a table and a couple of things of mine, testimonials and certificates framed on the walls.

"Pick a spot," I says.

"Sit on the couch," she says.

She takes a cassette from the fanny pack she's got around her waist and, after turning on the TV, stands there holding it in her hand.

"I know you hired Willy Dink to do a little camera surveillance at the murder scene," she says.

I don't say nothing, but my ears get pointed. She's the first one ever came right out and called Fay Wray's death murder.

"I know quite a bit about camera surveillance," she goes on. "Not from when I was a cop but since I've gone into the insurance business. The companies selling health care policies are all cherry pickers. They like to get people who are in good health and avoid preexisting conditions like the plague. I won't go into all the details, except to say that the policies I purchase for the members of my guild cover spouses and children, too. Because of Harry Hovannis's disability and the prospect of growing medical expenses for a helpless cripple, the premiums for Mavis's insurance would have been prohibitive."

"Who?" I says automatically, having forgot for a minute

there that it was Fay Wray's real name. "Oh, yeah, Fay Wray." I correct myself right away.

"I won't tell you how much I disliked her husband. He had his ass in a butter tub and he meant to suck her dry. After the way the bastard abused her the way he did. Well, I didn't believe he was as disabled as he claimed to be."

"Why was that?"

"He hit on me and let me know that if I agreed to having sex with him, I'd have no complaints about his ability to perform."

"That wasn't very smart."

"Who was it said that some men had all their brains in their cocks? Well, Harry Hovannis is certainly one of them."

I look at the cassette she's still holding.

"I know I'm hitting a long ball here, Jimmy, so maybe I should get right to it and answer any questions you may have after you see what's on this tape."

She puts it into the VCR and punches Play.

"It was a lot easier than I thought," she says.

I watch as Harry Hovannis comes out of his building over on Fullerton in the Thirtieth Ward. I watch as he wheels hisself down the street for ten, eleven blocks. I see him stop at a playground where some kids is shooting hoops. He sits there for a while. Then he takes the harness that holds his head in the cage off his neck and shoulders. He gets up out of the wheelchair and shakes his arms and legs. He wheels it into the playground and stashes it alongside the chain-link fence beside a bench where some big kids and young men are waiting for a turn on the court. He knows some of them and they exchange some silent greetings.

"I was across the street with a long lens," Mabel says.

"Weren't you afraid he'd spot you? I could see he was being careful."

"He didn't know anybody was watching," Mabel says.

"But I mean, a woman as big as yourself."

"I know how to carry myself like a man. I did it long enough," Mabel says, laughing a little. "Anytime I want to look like a man, it's not difficult. Here's a nice bit," she says.

Hovannis gets off the bench with two other guys and goes out on the court. They start a game, three on a side. He ain't the least bit afraid of body contact, shoving with his hands and making physical contact every chance he gets.

The tapes goes to snow.

Mabel stops the VCR and says, "So?"

"You think Hovannis did his wife?"

"I'd bet the family jewels on it, if I still had them."

"You show this tape to anybody else?" I asks.

She hesitates a long minute until I'm afraid she ain't going to tell me anything more.

"You have this tape before Fay Wray died?" I asks.

"Yes."

"And you knew about her and Lundatos?"

"I had my suspicions," Mabel says. "Little things she dropped in conversation. Bits picked up here and there. I was certain after I looked into her date book."

"So you called me because you wanted somebody to pay a price for what happened to her?"

"I figured everybody had something coming, one way or another," Mabel says.

"Lundatos some embarrassment and humiliation?"

"Why not?"

"Suppose he'd been charged with murder?"

"I'd have dropped this off with the cops long before it came to that. I wasn't going to let Hovannis walk."

"You was going to do the right thing."

"That's why I called you, Jimmy, to make sure it just didn't fall through the cracks or get covered up."

"So who got to you, Mabel? Who finally got to you?"

"They didn't get to me, Jimmy. Lundatos and his crowd got to Hovannis. He was threatening to bring a civil suit for unlawful death. He figured they'd try to pay him off big and he figured right."

"But he didn't figure on you and that tape."

"That's right."

"So you cut yourself a large piece of his action."

"Fay Wray was dead. I saw a chance here to do something for the other women."

I let her know by the expression on my face that I don't believe that for a minute.

"Nothing for yourself?" I asks.

"Sure, something for myself. I'm not a saint, Jimmy, and I've always been a pragmatist. Just like you. Were you ready to go to the wall on this one?"

"I didn't have the juice," I says.

She tosses the tape cassette into my lap.

"Now you got the juice."

She starts to leave the room.

"Why'd you change your mind, Mabel?" I asks.

"How the hell do I know? Maybe Milton Halstead could've told you."

31

So there was blackmail behind it after all.

Once his cover is blown, after we show the cops the tape of Hovannis playing basketball and Pescaro arrests him, it ain't long before Hovannis gives it up and tells us how it happens.

How he kept his recovery from his wife a secret so she wouldn't toss him out. How he asked her to put the money to pay the doctors and the therapists into a bank account he opened in his name so he wouldn't be embarrassed having to write out the checks so everybody'd know she was supporting him. Which, of course, she was. And how he just wrote out checks to hisself, ready to tell her, in case she asked, that the professional liked to be paid in cash. It wasn't much trouble to get some phony invoices made so she could keep her records straight, especially after Mabel Halstead put a bug in her ear about tax deductions and so forth.

When and how he finds out that Leo Lundatos is one of her clients, he don't say. But when he does find out, an idea starts cooking and he approaches her with a scheme whereby they can record some tapes and maybe even plant a television camera showing Lundatos and her in action which could be used to squeeze a payday so big out of Lundatos that she can give up the life and they can go off to some island in the Caribbean and live happy ever after.

She won't go for the recordings or the pictures. She's basically too decent for that sort of thing. However, even though she don't say yes, she also don't say no to trying for a smaller score by just threatening Lundatos in a small way about the possibility of public exposure.

Hovannis shows hisself to be the sort of snake what's got a hundred twists and a stinger in both ends.

He gets hisself a key to the door to the basement and also to the elevator, which has got another door to the cage in the back, concealed by fancy molding, because it's sometimes used to lift heavy deliveries of this and that to other floors besides the one on top. He goes to the trouble because he's thinking about planting a tape recorder and maybe a miniature camera in the bedroom whether his wife is in on it or not.

But first he'll let her make the approach to Lundatos and if the old Greek bites once, then Harry knows he'll bite again and again and again. Harry'd have his own automated teller machine. He could stand up out of that goddamn wheelchair. He could run out on the wife who'd sell herself to anybody with the price. Which is typical of a person loaded with guilt because somebody who loves them is willing to make such sacrifices.

So he goes over that morning, lets himself in through the basement and takes it up to the love nest, you want to call it that.

He rings the bell and she opens the door, wearing a Turkish towel robe because she's ready to take a bath.

She's surprised to see him sitting there in his chair and asks him how he got upstairs.

He tells her he took the elevator, which, apparently, somebody forgot to lock.

He follows her back into the bathroom and asks her if she made a deal with Lundatos.

She tells him she never agreed to blackmail Lundatos or anybody else. It was against her principles.

"She drops the bathrobe and steps into the tub," Hovannis says. "I'm thinking about how there was a time, when we was first married, that she was shy about doing something like that even in front of me, her own husband. I could see how brazen she'd become. It was nothing to her to walk around naked in front of strange men. To show her tits and bush to any sonofabitch who had the price. And she stands there washing between her legs where that fucking old Greek had been, talking to me about principles. Then all of a sudden she frowns and says she understands how I got into the elevator but how did I get up the little flight of stairs to the front door. So I stand up and show her how the fuck I did it. I tell her I'm sick and tired of her treating me like a lapdog. I'm not a lapdog. I'm her husband and I've made every effort to make myself whole again, with which I was going to surprise her when we were on our way to our new life. But she didn't care enough about that to squeeze a few dollars he'd never miss out of a crooked politician. She stood there naked, saying nothing, just staring at me with a look on her face like I was something she scraped off her shoe."

Hovannis said that he may have slapped her but wouldn't admit that he held her under the water until she drowned.

That would have to be settled in the courts.

He did tell how he waited until he was approached by an Irishman by the name of O'Meara and a cold fish in a three-piece suit who never gave him his name.

They were there to tell him that in a case like this, the cops would be looking hardest and longest at the husband of the deceased, but that he had nothing to worry about as long as he said, being a man confined in a wheelchair the way he was, that he had no idea what his wife was doing nights. So he told them that he did know and that he also had his wife's client list stashed in a safe place, but if there was any chance that somebody could provide him with the means of a modest living, being a man confined to a wheelchair, he'd even forget about where her body had been found.

So a deal was cut. Which might not have lasted very long. Which might have ended with Harry Hovannis falling under a six-wheeler or a municipal bus, being a man confined to a wheelchair and all.

Except Mabel Halstead walked into the picture and wanted a piece of the action.

And then changed her mind, maybe because she was the champion of the whores or because she'd been a cop in a previous incarnation.

Willy Dink tells me that with his new lifestyle, living in a wood butcher's van, no matter how unique and novel it might be, is no longer suitable. Would I keep my eyes open for a flat he might rent where the landlady wouldn't care if he kept a couple or three clean pets? I don't know if he's already three steps ahead of me, but when I mention we're going to rent the flat on Polk Street until we find a buyer in the great by-and-by, he jumps at the chance.

There's still a lot to do around the house on Aberdeen. Maybe a year's worth of work like Mary says, but I got a suspicion, a house this big, she's going to hand me a honey-do list every week and it ain't ever going to end.

Going over to the neighborhood where Janet asked the nuns to go do a little social work, I notice the hookers ain't left the stroll altogether but at least they're wearing blouses considerably higher and skirts considerably longer than they usually did. In fact it's even a little hard to tell which is which, these women chatting on the street, except the nuns is in black and don't wear makeup and the hookers are wearing colors and plenty of paint and eye shadow.

*   *   *

I finally got around to delivering Delvin's bequest, the tiepin like a gold knot with the diamond in the center, to the mayor.

He takes it from my hand and twirls it between his thumb and finger so the diamond flashes like a tiny sparkler.

"He was a grand old fella, was Chips Delvin," he says.

"Indeed he was," I says.

"So I understand you're living in his house on Aberdeen."

"I am."

"I understand Leo Lundatos has decided to retire from politics altogether and is prepared to back you big if you decide to run for alderman in the Eleventh."

"It's the first I heard about it," I says.

"Well, he made me his messenger, you see. He didn't want to make the offer before he knew for certain that you'd accept his endorsement. He's a proud man and easily wounded."

I nod, not being able to think of anything to say.

"You'll also have Johnny O'Meara's blessing," the mayor goes on.

I still don't say anything. He lets the pause build and then he lays the sword on my shoulder, making me one of his knights, if I choose to accept the honor.

"And you'll have my blessing, too."

Welcome to the Island of Morada—getting there is easy, leaving . . . is murder.

Embark on the ultimate, on-line, fantasy vacation with
MODUS OPERANDI.

Join fellow mystery lovers in the murderously fun MODUS OPERANDI, a unique on-line, multi-player, multi-service, interactive, mystery game launched by The Mysterious Press, Time Warner Electronic Publishing and Simutronics Corporation.

Featuring never-ending foul play by your favorite Mysterious Press authors and editors, MODUS OPERANDI is set on the fictional Caribbean island of Morada. Forget packing, passports and planes, entry to Morada is easy—all you need is a vivid imagination.

Simutronics GameMasters are available in MODUS OPERANDI around the clock, adding new mysteries and puzzles, offering helpful hints, and taking you virtually by the hand through the killer gaming environment as you come in contact with players from on-line services the world over. Mysterious Press writers and editors will also be there to participate in real-time on-line special events or just to throw a few back with you at the pub.

MODUS OPERANDI is available on-line now.

Join the mystery and mayhem on:
- America Online® at keyword MODUS
- Genie® at keyword MODUS
- PRODIGY® at jumpword MODUS

Or call toll-free for sign-up information:
- America Online® 1 (800) 768-5577
- Genie® 1 (800) 638-9636, use offer code DAF524
- PRODIGY® 1 (800) PRODIGY, use offer code MODO

Or take a tour on the Internet at
http://www. pathfinder.com/twep/games/modop.

MODUS OPERANDI—It's to die for.

©1995 Time Warner Electronic Publishing
A Time Warner Company